MW01135190

Frogs, Friends & Funerals

JOE SILVA

Nice Meeting You At The Big Apple!

Joe Silva

Frogs, Friends, & Funerals

Learn about the author, Joe Silva, by visiting the following website:

www.TheJoeSilvaWebsite.com

I dedicate this book to my children,
Tyler and Charline

And to everyone I called friend
during my life on earth

CHAPTER 1

Terry

The Funeral Director did exactly as his title suggested, of which he had done hundreds of times before, in a sadly short amount of time.

"Right this way, please," he softly said to the six pallbearers that convened, as instructed, in the funeral home's carpeted hallway before he oddly pivoted his body in the opposite direction on one heel. His other shoe crossed his leg like an elegant, or rather overly rehearsed, figure skater. Gliding along, he led them to the glass doorway at the end of the hall and lined them up, three on each side. Three steps down, a hearse that was about to carry their friend's body pulled up as their eyes fixated on it. Each had their own thoughts that silently bumped into each other's like autumn leaves surrendering to a foggy hurricane. The director secured the doors right on cue, and without making eye contact, he stated, "Stand here as the guests depart the home, and once the casket is wheeled over, you'll be given further instruction."

Each of the six friends turned their heads from the hearse, to the man who was briskly walking away from them. He stopped at a podium and microphone that was just outside the viewing room, and began to call the names of the guests so they may return to their cars for the funeral procession.

"Wait. That's it?" Hank asked. "We don't get to say goodbye to Terry?"

"Didn't you say goodbye when you knelt at his casket?" asked Benny.

"When I got here? No. I was saying hello to him. I figured that the goodbye would happen on the way out."

"I kind-of wanted to give a better goodbye, too," Charlie added.

"We can just go back in there quickly, after the people leave," stated Grant.

"Unfortunately, I think that we've all said our last goodbyes to Terry," Jenny suggested. "The family is the last to see the body."

A middle-aged couple exited the viewing room. The six pallbearers stood at attention, and the grieving man rubbed the woman's back while she patted her eyes with a tissue as they passed by.

"This just sucks," said Billy, as a slow parade of mourners began to trickle by.

Eventually, Terry's parents said their last goodbye to their son and headed down the hallway toward the limousine that awaited them near the hearse. As they began to pass by the more-than-familiar pallbearers, Terry's mother broke down and hugged Hank, weeping uncontrollably. Hank had been Terry's best friend since kindergarten. Billy was the next to weep hard, followed instantly by the rest.

Once Terry's parents made their way past the doors, Grant wiped his eyes and leaned his head around a dividing wall, which gave him a view of his friend's casket at the far end of the long room. A funeral home worker was turning a metal bar he had inserted through a grommet in the casket. As he rotated it, Terry's head sunk lower into the casket until his face disappeared from Grant's view forever. The worker walked to the opposite end of the casket and opened the lid that covered Terry from his waist down. He turned around, grabbed the blanket that all of Terry's friends had signed, which hung on a display that included photos of Terry, and haphazardly threw it into the casket before closing both lids and locking it shut.

"What a jerk," Grant said, breaking the somber silence. The others looked at Grant in a surprising manner. "The guy just threw Terry's blanket into the casket. Like, have some respect!" Grant's voice grew louder, and it looked as though he was going to confront the worker as he pushed the casket toward the pallbearers on a metal dolly.

Jenny grabbed hold of Grant's arm, giving a gentle squeeze. "No, Grant," she ordered, under her breath.

The thin, yet rugged blanket originally belonged to his father from his days in the Air Force, but it had been Terry's ceaseless possession for as long as any of his friends could remember. He suffered from a life-long disease, and constantly felt cold, so that blanket followed Terry everywhere. Although he appeared mostly normal to all of his friends, aside from the times they needed to carry him when he felt weak or out of breath, the blanket was a constant reminder that Terry had a shorter life expectancy and would most likely be the first of them to go, barring no unanticipated tragedies. Yet, even with that probability, Terry's death sent a shockwave throughout the gang. Time flew by, and one of them was already dead.

Frogs, Friends, & Funerals

The seating inside the pallbearer's vehicle included two luxurious benches that faced each other. Each of the friends stared uncomfortably outside, while taking turns glancing quickly at each other, hoping to not catch another's eyes while silently wondering who would be the next out of the group to go. Familiar scenery passed by as the funeral procession made its way through the town where they all grew up. Each street, business, forest, school, and baseball field, contained countless memories that evoked sadness and happiness all at once as they rode toward the cemetery.

"Why did we stop?" Charlie asked.

"We're at a traffic light," answered Billy.

"No. Charlie's right," Grant chimed in. "All other traffic is supposed to wait for funeral processions to pass by. We should have been able to have gone straight through the red light."

While they sat there in front of a car dealership, waiting for the light to change, a brightly colored inflatable character on the sidewalk appeared to repeatedly bend down toward the car and snap back up with flailing arms, as if to taunt the pallbearers inside while their collective attention was drawn to it.

"What do they even call those annoying things?" asked Billy.

"I think they're called Air Dancers," answered Jenny.

"I always thought they were called Fly Guys," offered Charlie.

"Aren't they called Tube Men?" Grant countered.

"I heard 'em called Breezy Geezers in the past," Benny added. "Either way, I agree with Billy and think that they are dumb. They are a distraction to drivers, and I'd bet that they cause a lot of accidents."

"When I die, I want one of them set up in front of the funeral home," Hank asserted.

"That would be pretty funny," Jenny said.

"That would be pretty dumb," Benny maintained.

"If I die before you, Benny, promise me that you will rent one for my wake."

"Yeah, right."

"I'm serious. Promise me right now in front of everyone that you'll rent one for me."

"I'm not renting-"

"White! Rent a white one. Like a dancing ghost."

"Whatever."

"Promise me right now."

"Chill, man. If it means that much to you, then fine. I promise. One stupid white whacky waving tube man coming right up."

"Not RIGHT up! I'm not planning on dying anytime soon."

12

"It's always sooner than you think," Billy added to the conversation.

The light turned green and Hank nodded to the inflatable dancing thing as the funeral procession continued on.

"Did you really just nod to it?" Benny grilled.

"Too bad they didn't have those when we were kids," Jenny added. "We could have had one of them at the end of Terry's driveway when we held that backyard carnival."

"Wow! Talk about a blast from the past," Grant responded. "How old were we?"

"I'm guessing that we were around ten," said Charlie. "Terry always said that it was his favorite memory."

Jenny began to cry silently, while looking out the window so as to not get noticed.

"I think that Terry spent half the day in the dunk tank," Grant recalled.

"Of course he did. It was like a hundred degrees that day and he kept jumping into the water from his perch, even when the people trying to dunk him missed the target," Benny detailed. "I think it was the only day in life that I saw Terry and he didn't seem to be cold."

"Didn't your Dad build that dunk tank, Jenny?" Hank asked.

When Jenny didn't answer, the others looked over and noticed that she was unsuccessfully trying to regain her composure, resulting in them losing theirs. A box of tissues circulated between the six of them until the procession pulled into the cemetery. When the car stopped, all eyes focused on the tarp of green artificial turf a hundred or so feet away, which covered the large mound of dirt that sat off to the side of an open grave that waited patiently for their friend's body.

The funeral director displayed less patience, as he walked up to the car and abruptly opened the vehicle's door to command his brigade of pallbearers. "Follow me to the rear of the hearse, three per side."

"Not so fast," Grant quipped, unapologetically. "That person in the hearse may be your customer, but he is our friend and we aren't going to rush him to his grave. We'll be out in a minute." Grant pulled the door closed, feeling a tinge of satisfaction from his words and sudden action, which he claimed to the others were warranted in the wake of the funeral home's disrespectful manner in which Terry's casket was closed. He held his right hand toward the center of the car's interior and said, "It's been too long since we've all been together. Before we carry Terry to his grave, let's promise here and now to meet-up at least once every two years."

Five hands stacked on top of Grant's hand, as each renewed their pledge of life-long friendship, just like they did throughout their early years.

Without mentioning it, each felt the void caused by the absence of Terry's hand in the stack.

"Well, I was going to wait until after the funeral to announce this, but I propose that our next gathering happens one year from this coming July, at which time I'll be getting married," Charlie announced.

"No WAY!" Jenny exclaimed. "That's great, Charlie. I'll be there!"

"Me, too!" said Benny.

"You know that I'll be there, Charlie!" Grant confirmed.

"You're finally getting married? Count me in!" Billy hailed.

"Well, one of us is getting married while another is getting divorced," Hank revealed. "But I'm happy for you, Charlie, and I'll make sure that I'm there."

"Aww, I'm so sorry, Hank," Jenny consoled. "Maybe I can be your date at the wedding."

KNOCK KNOCK...

"Reality is knocking," Grant said, while giving the funeral director a thumbs-up through the window. "Let's go carry our friend Terry one last time."

CHAPTER 2

Jenny

"I can't believe that you're actually here in Savannah," Jenny said, while unlocking the back of her SUV.

"Well, after going through the worst divorce in history, I figured I'd spend the last few cents to my name and get away from it all for a few days, and admittedly, to pick your brain so I can get a woman's perspective on what the heck just happened in my life," Hank replied, while tossing his duffle bag in the back of Jenny's vehicle.

"What happened? You married a psychotic you-know-what," Jenny boldly stated. "All of us knew it, but you know how it goes."

"How what goes?"

"How none of us could really say anything. You were so in love, and not about to listen to anyone who would potentially talk you out of marrying her."

"How could you tell early on that she was psychotic?" Hank asked, while clicking his seatbelt before Shelly pulled out of the airport parking lot.

"Seriously, Hank? The first time we all met her she had us participate in a séance to reach her dead former husband for his 'earth birthday', and the second time we got together was a few months later, in which she had us involved in yet another similar ceremony, but for his 'death birthday'. We knew then and there that you weren't ever going to be a priority in that lady's life, and if you couldn't blatantly see that for yourself, then none of us was going to successfully change your mind."

"Well, I wish one of you would have tried. You have no idea how badly that witch has ruined my life in such a short amount of time. I was ok with the birthday celebrations, though, especially at first. I mean, if it were me that had died, I'd want to be remembered, too."

"Remembering is one thing, obsessing and bringing in others that never knew him is quite another, especially when it comes to anti-Christian practices like holding séances and speaking through mediums."

"That IS another thing. She spent hundreds of dollars every single month to speak to him, and whatever her quote-unquote 'husband' said through the medium was the direction our life would have to take. What I don't get is how 'he' spoke so highly of me through that medium for four years, and then out of the blue, she wants nothing to do with me. What kind of psychic is that? If she was any good, the psychic would have called her out for being a psycho!"

"Don't beat yourself up over it, Hank. You're a smart man and a good guy. You'll be back on your feet in no time."

"I've got a feeling that it's going to take a very long time," Hank replied, while gazing out at the southern mansions that they were driving by.

"Financially speaking, you must have at least received half of the house and the business, right?"

"Not even close. She was defaming me so badly around town, and through our customers and to *my* friends, telling everyone that I was a widow-chasing-gold-digger. Because of that, I agreed to give her the house, the five acres of land, and the business, all in exchange for her paying the taxes that she messed up while cashing in her deceased husband's IRA's that she never told me about."

"Are you freakin' kidding me? You're the most generous soul that I know, and the LAST person who would *ever* dig for gold like that!"

"My lawyer thought I was crazy for conceding so much, but I just got such a sinking feeling in my stomach every time I heard someone in town repeat her lies about me that I wanted to prove her wrong. Hopefully, I'll just land another executive position with a corporation, like I had before I met her. It's just that I've been out of the industry for a few years while building our family business, that jumping right back in hasn't worked out for me as of yet."

"Where have you applied?"

"Where have I *not* applied? I sent out just over a hundred resumes since the week of Terry's death six months ago, which is when I learned that she wanted a divorce, along with the family business."

"And?"

"And just one interview from all of those resume submissions, and zero job offers."

"But, you were so successful as a business manager for some big-name corporations for almost two decades, plus owning your own business. Why wouldn't you get hired right away?"

"That's what I keep asking myself. Is it that I'm middle-aged and too old now? Too long out of the marketplace? Not up to date on the latest technologies compared to new college graduates? What I *do* know is that I am beginning to panic inside."

"What if you don't find something soon?"

"I've been slowly selling my material things to survive, and placing my trust in God, while sleeping on an air-mattress in my sister's unfinished basement. I guess I need to trust even more if I am feeling the onset of panic, though."

Jenny pulled up along the sidewalk in front of a row of federal-style brick houses that were built in the 1850's.

"Here we are," Jenny announced, while extracting her keys from the SUV's steering column before looking at Hank. "Aww," she reacted, when she saw his eyes welling up. "Hang in there, Hank. It will all work out. Come on in and I'll make us a nice dinner."

The next morning, the sun's rays peeked through the leaves of a large southern live oak tree, depositing their Spanish-moss-filtered light directly on top of a stack of Savannah tourism brochures that rested in front of Hank, atop a round and elegantly casted iron table. Although he brought them out to study in the shared courtyard between Jenny's home and the house that faced the next street over, Hank mostly ignored the brochures while he deeply contemplated something else.

Jenny walked over with two mugs of coffee and rearranged the brochures to allow space on the table for the two beverages. "So, did you decide what you'd like to visit first?"

"This huge tree appears to be situated precisely in the center of this courtyard. Do you own it, or does whoever lives in that house own it?" Hank questioned, without taking his gaze off the base of the tree.

"Isn't it strange, if you think about it, to consider one living thing being owned by another living thing?"

"When you put it that way, is does sound strange," Hank somewhat agreed before raising his coffee mug to his lips, and then returning it to the table before taking an actual sip. "But, when people have kids they don't really *own* them, yet society has an agreed upon structure that suggests that they actually are parents' possessions, at least until they reach adult age. You hear it all the time in public places when a child gets lost – "Who does this kid belong to?" for example."

"Hank, you think too much. Take a sip of your coffee and enjoy some mental down-time for a change," Jenny recommended.

"The thing is, when a kid does something wrong like breaking a window, the parent is expected to pay for it, even if it was an accident."

"What are you trying to say, Hank?"

"Who pays for the damage if a limb falls from that tree and hits one of the houses, or worse, kills a person?"

"Well, no amount of money will bring back the dead."

"But society sure loves to collect money upon one's death, whether it's the taxman or relatives. I mean, what even determines a person's life's value?"

"I guess it may depend on what kind of job they had, what their earning potential was, or if they had any kids?"

"So, are you saying that you and I have less valued lives because we have no kids, with mine having even less value than that because I currently have no job?"

"I don't know. Let's just say that insurance pays for it."

"Then who pays for the insurance policy on that tree, which is exactly half on your side of the courtyard, and half on your neighbors side?"

"Hank. Your coffee is getting cold," Jenny said, while rifling through the brochures, which she quickly placed in an empty clay flowerpot that rested on a brick partition near the table. "You know what? *I'm* going to be your tour guide today."

While Jenny showered, Hank explored the living room of her cozy home. At least half of the photos that hung on the walls were of various animals from the wildlife sanctuary where Jenny worked. He paused at a framed childhood picture of all seven friends at their middle school graduation. Leaning in to get a better look, he thought to himself that Terry did have a sickly appearance, even back then, compared to the others. He contemplated how nobody in their gang of friends ever even noticed. That eighth-grade graduation day seemed like yesterday to Hank, and yet a thousand years ago, all at the same time. The frame next to that one held a photo of their graduation party from high school. It was taken on the back deck of Jenny's house, where her parents held a barbeque for the inseparable friends before they headed out to various graduation gatherings, and their eventual separate ways at the end of that summer. Jenny's dog, Barnaby, was also in the photo and Hank recalled how he followed the gang wherever they went. Even that night of graduation, Jenny and Grant persuaded a bus driver to allow Barnaby, a medium-sized collie, to ride along while the gang of friends traveled on the off-hours school bus from party to party. The town's chief of police arranged for the school busses to shuttle graduating students from one celebration to another throughout the night so that all of the graduated celebrants, families and friends, would be safe that night, especially if anyone decided to partake in alcoholic beverages. Shaking his head from a disbelief that never left him, Hank remembered how one of his classmates was killed that night in a drinking & driving accident, just before the midnight breakfast that the chief had planned at the local parish hall.

He and the gang learned about the tragedy when arriving at the late-night breakfast, after their bus was diverted from the main route because of the accident. That person was the first from their class to go. The latest was Terry, and in-between the two were at least a dozen or so acquaintances that lost their lives for various reasons.

As Hank made his way around the room, he saw that the covering over a large birdcage in the corner was zipped shut. Glancing over at the ornate grandfather clock that stood at attention on the opposite side of the room, Hank decided that Jenny probably forgot to open it up before she jumped into the shower. Taking liberty, he unzipped the front panel of the canvas covering and flipped it back, resting it on top of the cage.

"Well, aren't you a pretty bird," Hank said, while sticking a finger through two metal bars of the cage and wiggling it around before extracting it quickly when he suddenly remembered some foggy story of someone that lost a finger to a parrot's strong beak. "Pretty birdie want a cracker?" he added, using his best parrot voice.

The large and colorful bird sidestepped on his wooden dowel perch, away from Hank. "Ok, I can take a hint," Hank said, before continuing his tour of the living room.

As he began to pass in front of Jenny's antique roll-top desk, an item caught Hank's peripheral vision. It was a clear plastic trophy box that held a baseball that was signed by Jenny's Little League team after they won the town's championship. Hank smiled while remembering how he convinced the league to accept Jenny as the first female baseball player, and that her team won the final game against Hank's team. Jenny had replayed that game's final out a thousand times, as did Hank. It was the last inning and Hank was up to bat. His team was trailing by one run and there were already two outs by the time Hank stepped up to the plate. A runner was leading off third base that could tie the game if Hank got a solid base hit.

His coach signaled him to not swing at the first pitch, but Hank swung away, hitting it high and deep out toward right field. Jenny was there to make the catch just as Hank was reaching first base. Jenny's teammates rushed toward her from the infield to celebrate the win, but Hank never stopped running when he saw Jenny catch the fly ball, and was the first one to reach her, lifting her high off the ground with a celebratory hug. Once they got back to their neighborhood and were saying goodnight, she had Hank sign the baseball, too.

"I LOVE CRAIG", a high-pitched voice declared from the corner of the room.

Startled, Hank turned his head toward the direction of the voice. The bird was aggressively swinging on a large hoop that was suspended inside his cage.

"I LOVE CRAIG", the bird repeated.

"It sounds like you and Mickey Macaw are getting acquainted with each other," Jenny said, as she walked into the room, brushing her wet hair.

"Yes, he's apparently opening up to me, but 'I love Craig'? Haven't you two been broken up for like two or three years?"

"Now you can hear firsthand why I never bring any guys home."

"Just because he says I love Craig now and then?"

"I LOVE CRAIG. I LOVE CRAIG."

"It gets worse," explained Jenny. "Mickey Macaw gets very jealous when my male friends spend the night, not that it is often, but he never does this when my female friends pull an overnighter."

"He must've loved Craig even more than you, to keep saying that."

"It's my fault," Jenny said, while opening his cage door to extract his empty fruit bowl. "I was

26

head over heels in love, and believed that Craig and I would be together forever. It was the first thing that I taught Mickey Macaw to say when I brought him here from the wildlife sanctuary. Big mistake."

"CRAIG. I LOVE CRAIG."

"Come on, he's not so bad that you can't have male company."

Mickey Macaw got louder and louder. *"SO MUCH! I LOVE CRAIG! I LOVE CRAIG SOOOO MUCH! CRAIG SO MUCH!"*

"This is embarrassing," Jenny chuckled.

"I think it's hilarious!" Hank laughed back.

"SOOOOO MUCH!"

The two friends walked along the brick sidewalk that followed a row of Federal-style brick homes, where each seemingly connected to the next. They reached a quiet intersection that posed as a gateway to other architectural styles, such as Romanesque with its arch & dome designs, Regency that offered triangular pediments and circular stairs, Greek Revival that is depicted by gabled portico, Second French Empire with turrets and vertical accents on building tops, and the Georgian style with hipped roofs and symmetrical square facades. On the other side of the street was a beautiful park with tree-lined walkways, well-manicured grass, fountains, and countless flower gardens surrounded by knee-high wrought iron fences. Above their heads, Spanish moss hung Omni-presently, and followed them like a subtle moon on a hazy evening, all while the sun tried to break through the few possibilities that the moss would allow.

"What a beautiful city," Hank expressed, while inhaling the late morning's florally fragrant yet humidity-heavy southern air, and gazing over at the park.

"It truly is, Hank," Jenny agreed. "I love it here. Hey, did you know that Savannah has over twenty parks like that one, each with its own name and story behind it?"

"Is that something I *should* have known?"

"Not necessarily. I just know how you like to research anything and everything."

"I didn't research Savannah. Knowing that you were here was all the knowledge I needed to make me want to jump onto a plane and visit."

"Aww," Jenny sighed, while affectionately bumping her shoulder into Hank's. "I can actually educate you a little bit on the parks. Almost every other block or square in the city is a park. They have been in place since the early 1800's, with some of them dating back as far as the 1700's."

"What about this one?" Hank quizzed her, curiously.

"This one's called Pulaski Square. It was designed in 1837, and named after the highest ranking officer to die in the American Revolution, Count Pulaski of Poland."

"Impressive tour guide."

"I'm not done! He was killed right here in Savannah in 1779. Up ahead there is Chatham Square, which is another lovely park."

"So, what's the scoop on Chatham Square?"

"I have no idea." Jenny laughed.

"Now that's deflating, Miss Tour Guide!" Hank joked.

"I only know about Pulaski because it is so close to my house, and the real estate agent kept throwing me factoids about the neighborhood to get me to buy the place."

"It apparently worked. How long have you lived here for now? Seven years?"

"It's going on nine, believe it or not. It's been seven since my folks moved down here, though. Time sure does fly by."

"I haven't seen your folks in forever."

"I'll show you their condo building. It's just up here past Chatham Square."

Hank stopped in front of a brick and iron archway that led to a carriage house behind a stately mansion. "I am just amazed at all of the different styles of buildings here. So many various styles, yet nothing seems to clash. Just a joy to look at, really."

Jenny looked up at the large dwelling. "I love those windows. You know, I never really looked at that house before now." She took a gander at the homes on either side of it. "You are right. So many styles, and yet they blend harmoniously together. If only people with different ethnicities and cultures could exist side by side as peacefully and beautifully."

"I am one who believes that they can, that *we* can, if we simply pay more attention to each other and less attention to those entities that try to manipulate or divide races, families, and even friends, for their own agendas or political gains," Hank offered.

"Come on, Hank. It can't be as simple as that," Jenny challenged, while examining and comparing even more buildings that were visible from where her and Hank paused on the sidewalk.

"You don't think so?" Hank asked, while commencing to walk. "Tell me, how many times have you walked up and down this street?"

"Definitely more than any of the other streets in Savannah, besides my route to the sanctuary, considering that my parents live right over here. I do need to confess, though, that I am usually driving to their place, in-between running to or from home and work."

"Running to or from," Hank said, seriously. "That's how they control you."

"How who con-?"

"They offer quick hypnotic sound bytes or video clips of what they want you to believe, knowing that the public is too busy trying to keep up with where they tell you the bar of society is set. The public has zero time for research and they know it."

"But, who are 'they'? I mean, how does it all relate to these magnificent houses?"

"You just admitted that you never really looked at that house until today. You've been here nine years and haven't noticed these huge structures that you have passed by on your most travelled route."

Jenny nodded cautiously, not knowing where Hank was going with it.

"Now, let's say that you decided to attend a town planning meeting because a developer was looking to put in a new neighborhood near your house. That developer only knows how to make box-shaped condo buildings that all look the same. During his slick presentation, he explains that his single design is the best fit, citing that mixing too many styles would be unheard of, too conflicting, and way too unattractive, even though proof of quite the opposite existed quite blatantly in town for a couple hundred years. The easily led public would most-likely accept the developer's undesirable plan because their lives were too busy to pick the right choice, even when the low-hanging evidence was ripe and dangling right in front of them. Slick tongues can deceive a slumbering public."

"Hank," Jenny tried.

"And VOILA! Savannah has an ugly new neighborhood that nobody paid any attention to until it was already built, and way too late to do anything about."

"Hank!"

"What?"

"You think way too much!" she stated, half jokingly. "OK, this is Chatham Square on the left, and that building on the corner up ahead is where Mom and Dad live."

"Let's stop in and visit!" Hank excitedly suggested.

"I wish we could but they headed back home for a few weeks."

"Isn't it funny how people consider home to be where they spent most of their childhood, even though they may have lived elsewhere for most of their adult lives?" Hank asked.

"Yeah, that is kind of weird, but I get it," Jenny responded, adding, "As a matter of fact, my folks chose this condo over others they had looked at, for the sole reason that it's on Barnard Street, which reminded them of our dog Barnaby. I think that they miss our childhood as much as we do. Do you ever regret not moving out of the old town?"

"Nah, but it's never too late, so one never knows. I just may, someday, but with all of the traveling that I've done, I don't feel like I've missed out on anything."

"Benny never moved either. Do you two still hang out all the time?"

"Much less than you would think. It's weird, a few years ago when he was going through his divorce, he spent so much time at my house. He must've eaten dinner at our table at least four nights per week," Hank shared. "But, now that I'm divorced myself, it's like pulling teeth whenever I ask him to meet up."

"Maybe he's just been busy with the supermarket?"

"That's what I used to tell myself, but there is something very different about Benny now. Whenever we finally do hang out together, he acts disengaged from the conversation, or from my company, in general, and never stays longer than an hour or so."

"I sure hope that Benny is okay behind the scenes. He did seem a bit off at Terry's funeral, but that was understandable. We were all off."

As the two friends crossed in front of Jenny's parents' condo building, Hank looked up at the tall Gothic stone columns, then over to the Historic Preservation plaque near the large, yet simple double doors. "Wow, built in 1842. Imagine all of the people that have walked through those doors over the years."

"Most of them will never be known by anyone living today or after," Jenny pondered out loud. "How sad is that? Although, many say that Savannah is the most haunted city in America."

"I disagree with the haunted part. Souls aren't sticking around once the body dies. God's design is way too perfect for that," Hank said, while moving his fingers across the smooth and weathered stone landing that the monstrous columns were resting upon. "So, what are your folks doing back home?"

"Unfortunately, my aunt's health has declined to the point where she can't live in her house alone anymore. Dad is trying to get her into a nursing home, both physically and mentally."

"That really stinks."

"It sure does. Before she knew it, the last memory happened inside that home that she lived in, and loved in, for over sixty years. Kids were born, games were played, meals were cooked, dinners and conversations were shared, holidays celebrated, milestones after milestones quickly came and left, followed by the grown children moving out, and then the passing away of Uncle George in his favorite chair. Now, besides the memories, she'll have little more than a small room with a dresser, bed, closet, television and toilet. That's it."

"That's sad."

"Since my parents left a few days ago, I've been wondering if my aunt got to do everything that she wanted to in life, learn all she could learn, see all she could see? And if she did, did she savor it all as it happened?"

"Good questions," Hank affirmed. "Do you savor the days? Every one of them? Or, are you like me on many days, focused on the bad stuff that happened or worried about some potential catastrophe that may or may not come?"

"I'll admit that I need to work on that," Jenny said. "My problem is that I need to let go and let God. I am constantly feeling that I need to be in full control of every situation, whether it's my parents being at arm's reach and planning their meals, or keeping all of those animals alive at the sanctuary while somewhat dictating what their existence should be like, right down to the words I want a talking parrot to say."

"In control. You mean, like you becoming the tour guide today?"

"Ugh! Yes! I don't know how to just go with the flow and simply enjoy life most days, if I'm to be honest."

"I do think one needs to have a balance, though. Sometimes, going with the flow will send you right off the edge of a waterfall. It depends on whose hand is on the spigot. God's or man's? We must be able to discern between the two, considering all of the deceivers in the world."

A Savannah trolley tour bus pulled up to a building a few hundred feet ahead of where Jenny and Hank were standing. Jenny watched an elderly man help his handicapped wife off the trolley. The woman struggled to straighten her back, neck, and head, to look up at the window on the second floor that her husband was pointing out to her with his cane.

"That's it!" Jenny exclaimed. "I'm letting go! Follow me," she said in a burst, while taking Hank's hand and hurrying toward the trolley bus as the elderly couple struggled to re-board it.

When they reached it, the driver explained how the Savannah tour trolleys stop at several touristic sites, and that they could jump on or off the trolleys at any stop throughout the day. He also went on to say that his particular trolley bus had a film crew riding along for a television segment. Once Jenny and Hank agreed to sign the film company's waiver, they boarded the tourist-packed bus.

The trolley pulled away from the curb, and a reporter holding a microphone explained that they would be picking up a famous Savannah-based author in a few blocks, who would be a special guest for the TV segment. A cameraman positioned himself behind the bus driver so that he could film the author walking onto the bus, and then pan over to capture the trolley-riding tourists' reactions. The trolley came to a stop, the reporter announced the author's name as he walked on, and the cameraman pointed his lens toward the riders just in time to film them asking each other if anyone had heard of him.

"Cut!" the reporter shouted out, before asking the aging author to step back out, and onto the curb. While the bus circled around one of Savannah's twenty-two parks in effort to loop back and pick up the author again, the reporter instructed the tourists as to how they should react when the celebrity re-boards the bus – "Now remember, when he gets on the bus you are super excited! Some of you should even gasp in surprise. You LOVE this author!"

The cameraman repositioned himself and began filming as the trolley bus again pulled up to the curb. The door opened and the author walked onto the bus while coughing.

"Cut!"

"This is pretty funny," Jenny chuckled, while the bus made another loop around the park for another take.

"This is pretty fake," Hank replied. "This is exactly what I was saying earlier. Mass media manipulating the masses."

Once the film crew was satisfied with the shot, the ride to the next stop took just over five minutes. Both Jenny and Hank studied the face of the author that nobody seemed to know. His demeanor was that of a depressed man, looking sad and worried as he slouched on one of the trolley benches by himself. Everyone was eerily silent. Eventually, the bus stopped outside the entrance of Bonaventure Cemetery and the cameraman stepped off the bus to film some footage of the cemetery's sign, and of the trolley bus passing through the entrance.

Jenny and Hank waited patiently for the elderly couple to exit the bus before them. Once off the bus, Hank looked at the graves that could be seen as far as he could see in any direction. Some were large and elaborate, while others barely peeked over the grass that grew above the bodies that were buried long ago. The two friends 'went with the flow' and trailed behind the pack of tourists, the small film crew, and the so-called celebrity author. Feeling bad for the elderly couple, Jenny and Hank painstakingly walked slowly enough so that the turtle-speed elders felt that they were still part of the group.

Up ahead, the reporter rehearsed a few scripted lines with the author as they approached a specific grave. Once everyone caught up, the reporter told each of the tourists where to stand before the camera rolled for multiple takes of the staged graveside narration.

Powdering her nose before pulling the author closer to her by grabbing his arm, the reporter counted backwards from three and then looked at the camera to begin her rhetoric about being with the (not-so) famous author in one of the world's most beautiful cemeteries. That parlayed into a story of a young girl, whose fenced-in grave the tour group had assembled around. The author and the reporter alternated sentences as they told the story of the six-year-old girl who died from pneumonia more than a hundred and twenty-five years before. Legend had it that she had been haunting Savannah ever since. Due to the author's frequent coughing, or flubbed lines from the reporter, they re-shot the scenes so many times that Hank mouthed their scripted lines in an effort to get Jenny to laugh out loud in a cemetery. The cameraman caught Hank's antics in the background of what would have otherwise been the perfect take, which they would have used for the TV segment. He explained it to the reporter, who in turn repositioned Hank and Jenny to just outside the view of the lens. Hank spoke up and asked what the segment was for, and the reporter explained that it was for a story that would air on Halloween.

"Halloween?" Hank responded. "It's not even Easter yet. We're all set."

Hank put his arm through Jenny's and started walking back toward the trolley bus. The elderly couple followed suit, and the four of them together stopped along the way at a few other graves that hadn't received a single visitor in over one hundred years.

"That's not your mother's grave, Eleanor," the elderly man clarified to the woman, while she was rubbing the top of a gravestone. "Same last name. Maybe a distant cousin, but it's not Mother. Her grave is on the other side of the cemetery, but I don't think that the trolley will be going there."

Jenny and Hank looked at each other, then back at the confused woman. "Your mother is buried here at Bonaventure?" Hank asked.

The woman looked at Hank with a blank stare, and then back toward the gravestone.

"I'm sorry," the woman's husband reacted. "My wife gets bouts of Dementia. But, to answer your question, yes. Eleanor's mother was interred here almost seventy-five years ago, when Eleanor was just a child."

"I will personally see to it that we visit your mother today, Ma'am," Hank promised.

Jenny, Hank, and the elderly couple slowly made their way back to the trolley bus, well ahead of the other tourists, who were still being held hostage by the film crew, only because they felt that they needed to do everything that the production company told them to, which included collectively reading a poem at the young girl's grave that some believed would raise the dead, all for the camera that kept rolling for the staged segment.

At first, the trolley driver resisted making another non-scheduled stop for the aged couple, stating that he already stopped the trolley for them so they could look at one of their childhood homes. Hank had decided that he wasn't going to take no for an answer, and the driver finally agreed to stop at the grave of Eleanor's mother, once the others returned to the bus.

"That is so sweet, yet sad, at the same time," Jenny said, while watching the couple through her trolley window. The man placed his leisure suit jacket on a moss-covered bench near his wife's mother's gravestone. The elderly woman sat down upon it, grabbed hold of a cross that hung around her neck that her mother had given to her for her fifth birthday, and mouthed a prayer.

As the trolley finally passed through the exit gate of the cemetery, Jenny and Hank could overhear the elderly man trying to explain to his wife why her name was also engraved on the gravestone, telling her that her father purchased an extra plot there in case she wanted to be buried with them someday. He spent the next several minutes trying to convince her that they would, indeed, have their own grave together when their time would arrive.

Savannah Botanical Garden was the next stop along the trolley's route. The driver announced that they would be stopping there for five minutes only, but that another trolley would be along in thirty minutes for those who wanted to spend some time exploring its trails and vegetation.

"I'm going to use the ladies' room," Jenny said. "Don't let the trolley leave without me."

Hank waited for Jenny to walk into the restroom building, and then dashed into the gift shop next to it, returning with a plant before Jenny returned. A few minutes passed and Hank heard the air brakes releasing as the trolley driver closed its door.

"Wait!" Hank shouted. "My friend is still in the restroom." He heard the reporter and film crew grumble behind him about the delay. Hank turned around and said, "What's the rush? We all waited patiently for you to get your staged propaganda footage. You've got months ahead of you to edit it before Halloween even gets here. Smell the God-given roses for once."

Just then, Jenny returned, and the driver set the trolley bus into motion as she took her seat next to Hank, sensing that something just occurred.

"Nothing," Hank assured, knowing how Jenny could always read his face. "You bought yourself a rose?" he asked.

"It's for Eleanor," Jenny answered, before reaching her arm across the aisle and handing it to the frail woman. "I saw that your mother's gravestone had a rose etched on it, and I'd like for you to have this."

Eleanor held the flower up to her nose and inhaled. Her eyes closed, her lips formed a smile, and a tear rolled down her wrinkled cheek.

"What are you thinking about, Ellie?" the elderly man asked his wife.

Breathing in the scent of the rose a second time, Eleanor finally answered, "Oh, Robert! I can remember it as if it were just this morning, standing on a bench in Mother's rose garden, helping her hang laundry out to dry on the clothesline." Inhaling again, she continued, "I can hear her gentle voice singing hymns to me. Oh, what a beautiful day!"

Listening in, Jenny closed her eyes and shed a tear of her own. Hank was confused as to why Jenny would be crying, having not been aware of Eleanor's reaction to the rose.

"What's wrong, Jenny? Are you thinking about your aunt? Not feeling well?" Hank inquired caringly, while rubbing Jenny's arm.

"I'm ok, Hank. Sometimes, beautiful moments make me cry."

Hank looked over at Eleanor, who was basking in contentment while her husband looked lovingly upon her face. Jenny crinkled her forehead and breathed deeply, herself. She quickly opened her eyes, looked behind her, and then forward again.

Curious about Jenny's movement, Hank gave Jenny a look.

43

"Do you smell that?" Jenny asked. "It reminds me of the town library, back when we were kids."

"*That's* the scent!" Hank said to himself, in discovery. "I was wondering why it reminded me of you, Jenny." Hank reached down near his feet and picked up the plant that he purchased. "Here, I got this for you," he said, handing her the plant. "Last night, during dinner, you mentioned that you missed the snow that we had every winter back home. I thought that it could be your own little patch of snow in your courtyard."

"That's *right*!" Jenny said excitingly. "The library had flowers like this lining the walkway to the front door, and I remember always thinking to myself that the white flowers looked like snow on the ground in the middle of summer. Aww, thank you, Hank! You are so thoughtful. This is perfect because I have an empty flower pot in the courtyard that this plant is absolutely destined for."

"Next stop will be Forsyth Park," the bus driver announced.

"This is where the famous fountain is. Savannah is known for it," Jenny said. "Water has been flowing through its veins since the mid-eighteen-hundreds."

"So, you *do* know your Savannah parks," Hank chuckled.

As the bus came to a stop, Eleanor leaned across the aisle and asked Jenny if she would snap a photo of her and her husband at Forsyth Fountain.

"I would love to," Jenny responded.

Hank carried Jenny's plant as the four new friends exited the bus. Eleanor clung onto the handrail with one hand, while her other hand struggled to steady the flower under her nose. A rose petal shook loose from its bud and landed on the sidewalk from Eleanor's shaky hand movement.

"Oh my," Eleanor reacted, stopping in her tracks to look at the fallen petal.

"There are plenty more still on the stem, my dear," her husband, Robert, assured. "Let's keep walking so we don't hold this fine couple up."

Having been the last of the four of them to step off the bus, Hank made sure that everyone had their belongings, and then informed the driver that they would catch one of the later trolleys. Savannah's early-afternoon warm and muggy air filled his lungs as he acclimated away from the trolley's air-conditioning. Seemingly from every direction, the loud but uniformed hum of cicada bugs competed against the Southern humidity for the attention of every pedestrian.

"We're in no rush at all," Jenny said. "This is one of my favorite places in all of Savannah," she added.

"Ours, too," Robert stated. "Eleanor and I got married in front of the fountain sixty years ago today."

"Are you serious?" Hank asked. "Happy Anniversary!" he exalted.

"I am serious, and thank you," the elderly man responded. "God sure blessed me with the most amazing wife."

"That's wonderful," added Jenny. "I bet that you two spend a lot of time here at the fountain."

"It's been decades since we were here. I got stationed out west when I was in the service, and we ended up raising our kids out there. They gave us a trip to visit back home as our anniversary present."

"How nice of them. Did they travel out here with you?" Hank asked.

"Unfortunately, no. They are too busy with their own lives and couldn't join us. Sadly, our children are now scattered around the country, and as much as we try to organize a family reunion, they always seem to have other plans."

While the four of them continued with their slow walk toward the large and beautiful fountain, silence fell upon them for a moment. Even the loud insects went silent, all at the same time, adding attention to that brief span of time. Each took a few seconds to sort through some personal thoughts during that instant. Jenny studied the woman's frail body and slightly hunched posture, whose feet slowly inched closer to that significant piece of her past, and she wondered how many days of a future the woman had left... Hank contemplated never having kids of his own, wondering if he should have felt less concerned about it than he had been, considering that Robert and Eleanor do have kids yet hardly ever see them... Robert thought about their wedding photo, which was taken at the fountain right after the ceremony, in which his bride looked as beautiful as a model, and how he was handsomely dressed and in great shape. His mind raced through the years for any evidence of time bringing them to the frail state that they found themselves suddenly at, considering neither of them even noticed as it was happening... As for Eleanor, she pondered the fact that she actually accepted the elderly condition that time had brought her to, while still inhaling the scent of the rose and wondering how many steps she had left in life. If they were pre-numbered, and if Eleanor knew what that number was, she considered how she would simply find a way to walk even slower than she already was. Eleanor loved living life, and didn't want to ever leave Robert. She loved him just as much as she did on their wedding day, and possibly even more. Frustratingly, her limited body language and word usage were preventing her from expressing that as much as she wanted to. Robert's words and actions, on the other hand, allowed for all in his presence to get an idea of the immense depth of his love for his life-long, one-and-only, Eleanor.

When they finally arrived at the fountain, Robert bent over and kissed his wife. She responded by pulling the rose away from her face so she could place both arms around her husband. The elderly couple held their embrace for what seemed like several minutes to Jenny and Hank, who decided to sit on a nearby park-bench to give them some time alone so that they may reflect on their sixty years together as husband and wife. Eventually, Eleanor asked Robert to give their camera to Jenny so they could have their photo taken in front of the fountain one more time, six decades later.

While the couple stood arm-in-arm in front of the fountain, Jenny said, "Say Cheese - Say Anniversaryyyyy," even though the two elders were already flashing the perfect smile.

After taking several photos, Jenny asked Robert if he would be willing to do the same for her and Hank, while handing him his camera back, and then offering her phone that she had already set to camera mode.

"I'll do my best," Robert responded, while accepting Jenny's phone with tremulous hands of his own. After a few attempts, he handed the phone back to Jenny. "I think I got a few. Go ahead and check to make sure that they are ok."

Jenny scrolled through the photos on her phone that Robert took of her and Hank. The only photo that wasn't blurry was one of their knees and feet. "These are perfect," Jenny kindly said.

Eleanor signaled Jenny and Hank to join her and Robert on the park-bench. Noticing that neither of them was wearing a wedding ring, she asked how long they had been together for.

"Since kindergarten," answered Jenny, "But we aren't a couple. Just the best of friends."

"Ah," Eleanor responded, while looking at her rose.

"True friends are a gift from God. I hope that you always treasure that," Robert offered.

"We sure do, Sir. There are seven of us in our gang of childhood friends," Jenny explained.

"Well, six of us since Terry passed," Hank added.

"Life on earth is short," Eleanor slowly stated.

"I can vouch for that," Robert agreed, "whether a person dies at age one, or age one-hundred. For example, I can still see our wedding party, clear as day that assembled here sixty years ago. It feels like it could be yesterday."

"Will you celebrate with any of those folks that were here on that special day?" asked Hank.

Robert gazed over at the fountain with a remorseful look on his face and answered, "No. Some have passed away since then, and we don't speak to the others anymore."

"I think it's sad when people lose touch with each other," Jenny said.

"It wasn't so much that we lost touch. Over the years, our friends eventually did or said something that hurt or disappointed us. We found that by the time we were in our seventies, we were out of who we thought were our true friends," Robert explained.

"That's too bad," Hank said.

Another petal fell from Eleanor's rose, landing on her lap. "I just wish we had forgiven instead of ending our friendships with them," she said, while picking up the rose petal and rubbing it between two fingers, as if trying to hold onto something that she lost long ago.

Everyone thought that Eleanor had more to say, but she looked straight ahead at the fountain and said nothing. Eventually, she began to giggle.

"Where is your mind roaming to now, Ellie?" her husband asked, even though he already knew her answer, while grinning widely in reaction to seeing his wife so happy.

"My mind is right here," Eleanor replied, as her eyes began to dart back and forth from the fountain to various points in the park.

Robert looked over at Jenny and Hank and explained, "Eleanor's mind is right here in the park, thinking of when she was a young girl. This place is the foundation of her life's memories. Mine, too. It's where our friends and we learned all of the important things. Oh, we didn't realize it at the time because we were too busy having fun. We've returned here in our minds thousands of times throughout our adult lives, whenever we needed an escape, a reminder, a laugh, a cry, or just to feel that initial joy of life again. If you ask me, the key to a good life is having a strong faith in God, and having a place from your childhood to run back to, mentally, no matter what the world may throw at you."

At once, Jenny and Hank looked at each other and said out loud, "The frog pond!"

CHAPTER 3

The Frog Pond

The frog pond was smack-dab in the middle of a four hundred acre wood, which was located in the center of town. To those seven friends, it was more like the center of the galaxy. Jenny's father introduced the neighborhood kids to the frog pond when they were studying the amphibian in the first grade of school. Every year throughout their elementary ages, her Dad would lead a hike on the first day of spring from Jenny's yard, which abutted the forest, and a pathway to the pond. When they reached their destination, Jenny's father would count to three and the kids would shout "WAKE UP FROGGIES!" After that, he would allow the friends to explore the natural wonderland from the pond's shallow banks. There would be a search for any early tadpoles that may have been active, and each of the friends were hoping to be that year's first person to shout, "I found one!"

As soon as one of them declared the discovery, all of the others would gather around that spot to see for themselves. Jenny's father would give a short lesson on the early development of frogs, and then he'd award that year's winner with a book about the animal. There would be additional hikes throughout each year to the frog pond, where some of the frogs got to be as large as crab apples by August, but that first hike in spring was always ceremonial. The day carried the equivalent clout to any established major holiday.

Once the friends were ten years old, they had permission to take the path to the frog pond on their own. Everyone gathered at Jenny's house on the first day of spring that year with additional excitement in their hearts, and a tinge of nervousness in their tummies. Jenny's father stood with the children in the backyard and reviewed the rules of the forest with them. He gave Jenny a whistle in case they found themselves in any trouble, and gave each of them a library card so that they could be rewarded with books all summer long, regardless of who won the tadpole contest.

Several trails extended from the frog pond, each offering a unique destination and experience, with the town's library being at the end of one of those paths. Having grown up in town himself, Jenny's father recognized the value that the forest offered a childhood, and he knew the day would come when he would set the children free to explore, grow, and live. Over the past several years, he had led the kids on numerous hikes, showing them each and every one of the paths so that they could know those woods like the backs of their hands. But, for that first independent adventure, Jenny's Dad limited them to the frog pond and the library only. He informed them that he would eventually head out into the woods himself, just in case any of the kids spotted Jenny's cautious father keeping a watch on them from a distance.

The air still had a chill to it, as it did on mostly all of their past frog-wakeup holidays. Each of the friends was still wearing their winter coat, and Terry had his trusty blanket draped over his shoulders. Tree branches, leaves, and other forest debris peppered the trail, giving evidence that the woods endured its share of wind and heavy snow that winter. As the gang of friends made their way along the path, each did his or her best to jockey into the lead position, with every one of them feeling a sense of pride in knowing "their" woods.

By the time they reached the pond, the kids determined that Jenny would continue her father's tradition of counting to three before the wake-up shout.

"Hang on, Jenny," Terry said, while holding his hand out in front of the group. "Let's stack hands, that we can only wake up the frogs when all of us are here. If not, we wait until we can all be here, together."

"I'm in!" said Hank, placing a hand on top of Terry's.

"Me, too," added Benny, who added a hand above Hank's, followed by hands of the others.

"Are we ready?" Jenny asked, while looking at her circle of friends. "One, Two, Three."

"WAKE UP FROGGIES!"

That day kicked-off the best spring and summer of their young lives... well, until the next year's frog pond season, and the several years of them that would follow. For the gang of friends, every sunny summer day began at the frog pond, of every year, up until they graduated from high school. Typically, they would each meander around the pond until all of them had arrived. There were plenty of things that they could do to keep them occupied while waiting for the last of the friends to show up. The pond itself wasn't extremely large. It was rectangle in shape, and smaller than a quarter of a football field. In one corner of it were remnants of a small stone foundation, left behind by Trappist Monks a century earlier when the forest was part of a monastery. It made for a unique holding tank within the pond, where it was easier for the kids to catch the jumping frogs or fast-swimming tadpoles by hand.

A dirt walkway circled the pond's banks, and if they wanted to walk completely around it, they would need to traverse the small brook that slowly bled from the pond. At least a few of the friends would bleed every season, too, if they didn't negotiate the makeshift bridge carefully enough during a crossing. Sometimes it was a log or a branch that they would walk across, over the gap of stones and running water. Other times, if their bridge was washed away after a big rain, or ruined by other kids from town, the friends would cross the small ravine on a dare to learn who could make it to the other side by jumping. Inevitably, one or two wouldn't make it at one time or another, resulting in scraped knees and wet pants and shoes. Nobody headed back to their house when it happened to them, though, but rather they would deal with it on the spot so as to not miss out on that day's adventure.

'Rock Paper Scissors', or some other random-eliminating sort of game usually determined daily adventures. The last friend standing would get to choose which path of the forest they would follow first. Each friend had their favorite path, and although their path of choice may have changed by the time they graduated high school, it was evident that their lives were impacted by them.

Jenny's favorite path was the one that led to the town library. It seemed that whenever she came across an animal or plant that she hadn't seen before, she was off to the library to do some research on the subject. That particular path was also Grant's favorite in his younger years because the media room in the library would show a few movies each week during the summer. Grant was a big movie-buff for as long as any of the gang could remember, so they knew that if he won 'Rock Paper Scissors', they'd be heading down that path to watch a film. By the time Grant was in the eighth grade of school, he would toggle between the library path and the path that led to the cliff at the far end of the woods that overlooked the deep quarry. He could watch the massive dump trucks and excavating machines for hours, as they chipped away at the semi-circular stone-faced cliff that the friends would sit on top of.

As for Charlie, he would always lead the others down the path that went straight through the large field that existed in the forest. He always wondered why no trees ever took residency there, but he was grateful for the wide-open space.

Charlie's parents would donate a kite for each friend every year, and Charlie was always eager to fly them with the others. Teaching them the best flying methods if anyone had issues getting their kite into the air, and/or keeping it up there, was just as enjoyable to Charlie as flying his own. He loved the open sky that the field provided, mostly because he loved the thought of flying. Whenever he heard an airplane overhead, he would stop whatever he was doing and stare at it until it disappeared past the tree line.

Although it scared him early on, Terry's favorite path led to the 'Nine Men's Misery' hill. It was where Native Americans killed nine Colonists during the King Philip's War in 1676. On top of the hill sat a stone cairn to mark the spot of the slayings, along with a weathered metal plaque, which gave some information about the gruesome event that dated back almost four centuries. Terry really took to the subject of history in school, and he studied about 'Nine Men's Misery' in depth. His knowledge of its storied past earned Terry a Boy Scout merit badge, first place in his school's history fair, and the reputation of being the geek of the group, a title that he carried proudly within the forest, and outside of it. He would often have the others imagine what that day was like almost four hundred years earlier, as he narrated what happened there while they sat on the stone monument. Looking around in every direction, they would imagine the natives circling them on top of the hill. Sometimes, their own games of Cowboys and Indians would break out on that notable spot where one of the earliest, and actual, Cowboys and Indians tournaments played out.

That section of the woods was riddled with Beech trees. Several of them included names, initials, symbols, or dates carved into their smooth trunks, offering any hikers that may have walked past, some clues of a more recent history that dated back fifty or so years. During one of their early hikes, Jenny's father had pointed out the initials of his and his wife's names, which they had carved on one of the trees the day that he asked her to marry him, a couple of decades earlier. He had explained that carving into the trunks of trees wasn't something that he condoned, as the trees would be wearing those carvings like a tattoo for the rest of their lives, which would most-likely be longer than any of theirs. He had each of the friends promise to make only one carving in their lifetime, if they were to do it at all, and that it should represent something that they truly believed strongly in. The friends stacked hands in agreement. They added more to the pledge, saying that they would do their best to monitor against any visitors that tried to carve profanities onto the trees, of which there were already a few.

Of all the friends, Benny seemed to enjoy eating the most, so it was no surprise that his path of choice was the one that led directly to the loading dock of the town's supermarket. A few times per week, the gang would pool any loose change together that they may have earned by doing extra chores around the house, or from cutting a neighbor's lawn, and Benny would lead them to the store where they would load up on candy or chips.

If Benny won 'Rock Paper Scissors', but nobody had any money, he would still lead them to the supermarket where a friend or two would keep watch while Benny jumped into the dumpster, looking for any treats that may have been discarded because of an overdue expiration date. The kids couldn't believe how much perfectly good food was thrown away, daily. Once, when they were teenagers, Benny found frozen pepperoni pizzas in the dumpster. Grant ran home to find some matches, and by lunchtime they had started a small campfire near the frog pond. They were unsuccessful in keeping their pizzas above the flames long enough to actually cook them, but they ate the mostly raw food anyway. Within an hour, their fun in the forest was over, as each of them found themselves hunched over toilets in their homes for the rest of that day.

Frogs, Friends, & Funerals

Hank enjoyed whatever he and his friends did, regardless of which path was chosen for that day. His favorite activity over all others was playing baseball, but none of the paths from the frog pond went to a baseball field. The closest path was the one that headed to the library, with a baseball diamond diagonally across the street from the library's long driveway. It had bleachers, a scoreboard, snack stand and all. Sometimes, he would choose to take his friends there if he had won the choice of path for the day, but he often chose to have an adventure within the forest. The reason for that was he just wanted to be around his gang of friends, and most of the kids didn't enjoy baseball as much as Hank did. They would often use an excuse like they couldn't find their glove, or a parent didn't want them crossing the street to the ball field, even though none of the others actually asked their parents for permission, except for Jenny. She loved the game almost as much as Hank did. Jenny's father didn't hesitate to give her the green light to cross the town's main street in effort to play some baseball. He saw something in Hank's abilities, and love for of the game. The fact that Hank bought her a new baseball glove with his winter driveway shoveling money was also very much appreciated by Jenny's dad.

Hank's one-on-one time on the field with Jenny resulted in her being one of the better ball players in town by the time they were old enough to play on a Little League team. Hank was convinced that she was the best outfielder in town, although he never bragged about having a hand in her advanced skills. He just loved having a friend who could keep up with him on the baseball field, but it was the certain smile she would flash whenever she made a spectacular catch that he loved most of all.

Billy was the musician of the gang. His single-parent mother worked a few jobs to make sure that her and her children had a roof over their heads, food in their tummies, and private lessons for one thing that each of her children had a passion for. Billy's passion was the saxophone. The first instrument that Billy's mom was able to afford included a few dents, and a couple of bent keys and levers. The challenging condition of it made Billy work harder at playing it, resulting in him being an advanced player at a young age.

Living in an apartment with his mother and siblings didn't allow Billy to practice at home. The walls were paper thin, and the tenants on either side of his apartment worked and slept during odd hours. Instead, Billy would set aside an hour and a half every day to walk down the path that led to the old scouting camp stage, where he'd rehearse musical scales and songs on his sax. The days that he won 'Rock Paper Scissors', he would lead the others to the stage, where he would host a makeshift talent show. Each friend would need to come up with an act. Thanks to Billy's uncle for replacing the stage's rotted floorboards when needed, that stage served many purposes over the years. Grant even honed-in his acting skills during the year that he filled out his school schedule wrong and ended up in the drama class.

As for Jenny's dog, Barnaby, he followed the gang down any path that they would take. The only time he would venture off was if he wanted to have some fun chasing a squirrel through the woods. He also acted as a guard for the gang of friends, giving a warning bark if any strangers happened to be walking through the forest, or the time that he tried to stave off a roaming skunk and got sprayed by it. By the time the kids brought him back to Jenny's house, they all smelled like skunk, too.

Thankfully, Barnaby was walking with Hank near Nine Men's Misery one autumn afternoon when they came across the school bully and his sidekick. Hank noticed that the bully was carving profanities into one of the Beech trees. He was nervous about saying anything to him in effort to get him to stop carving, but he and the gang stacked hands on the topic and Hank knew that he needed to intervene. With a nervous quiver in his voice, he asked nicely for the bully to stop chiseling bad things into the trunk of the tree, which made him carve faster and deeper with his pocket knife. When Hank asked a second time, the bully turned around and asked him what he was going to do about it. Hank explained how it wasn't right, and that people who walk through the trails shouldn't have to see the filth that he was permanently branding into the side of the tree.

"Maybe I don't want to see your face," the bully said. "You don't own these trees, so beat it before I beat you!"

"No. I think that you should put your knife away and get out of here," Hank insisted, as his nervousness turned into anger.

"Oh YEAH?" the bully taunted. "I'll tell you what. I'll put my knife in my pocket just long enough to pummel you into next week!"

While the bully folded his knife, Hank could hear the faint sound of a saxophone coming from the stage area, two paths over. While the bully's friend positioned himself behind Hank, and the troublemaker began walking toward him as he slid his knife into his pocket, Hank began to scream for back up. "Billy! Hey, BILLY!"

Unfortunately, Hank's calls for help went unheard, as Billy continued to practice a piece of music. Barnaby sensed that something wasn't right, and began to bark at the bully.

"Oh, is your guard dog going to protect you?" the bully asked, just before throwing a punch at Hanks face and knocking him to the forest floor.

Barnaby, having been trained to never bite a human, continued to bark, even louder, as he darted away from the scene.

"Aww, it looks like your guard dog is nothing but a scaredy-cat," the troublemaker sneered, while Hank stumbled as he got up from the ground.

Hank struggled to regain his orientation, and the bully's sidekick got down on his hands and knees, just behind him. The bully pushed Hank back, resulting in him tumbling over the back of the sidekick and hitting his head on a log. The bully then jumped on top of Hank, punching him again in the face. Hank maneuvered his leg just enough to knee the bully in the crotch, forcing him to keel over in pain, although still trapping Hank under his overweight body. Dazed from hitting the back of his head on a log, and the front of his face being punched, Hank's consciousness was less than thirty percent when he heard Barnaby's footsteps in the brush around him.

While still trying to make sense of the situation, Hank could see his attacker reach into his pocket and pull out the pocketknife that he was carving with. The bully extended the blade from its casing and raised it above his head before going through with his on-the-spot plan to stab Hank. Just then, Billy's saxophone came down hard on the back of the bully's head, knocking the troublemaker out cold.

Barnaby began to bark again, as he ran from the scene for a second time. Billy kicked the unconscious perpetrator off Hank, while his sidekick ran away in fear. Within minutes, Jenny's father arrived at the scene, led by Barnaby. Soon thereafter, emergency workers bandaged the skulls of both boys before carrying the bully away for an ambulance ride to the hospital. The police got involved and the bully was placed into a correctional school for boys after his head healed.

Hank never forgot about how Billy and Barnaby saved his life that afternoon. He bought Barnaby the largest bone treat he could afford, and promised Billy that he'd find a way to repay him someday. That someday came a few years later, during the summer right after their high school graduation.

CHAPTER 4
Billy

One of the last events held on the stage in the forest was when Jenny practiced her Valedictorian speech in front of the gang a week before they graduated high school. It was a bittersweet moment, celebrating Jenny's amazing achievement, yet realizing that it indicated the summer would be their last season all together before most of them headed off to college. Terry shed a tear while the friends applauded Jenny's speech, in which she integrated each of them.

Jenny took a quick bow, and then noticed that all of them had wet eyes.

She jumped off the stage, put her hand out, and then said, "Let's stack hands that no matter what, we enjoy the best summer ever, and make it a point to return here whenever we are home for holidays."

All friends piled hands on top of the next, each one knowing that they experienced the greatest childhood that any kid could hope for.

As it turned out, Billy was the first to leave town, only two weeks after graduation, missing most of that last summer together. None of the friends expected it. Not even Billy himself.

Billy's departure stemmed back to the spring of sophomore year, when a high school dance troupe and steel drum band from St. Thomas spent two weeks at the gang of friends' high school, as part of a student exchange program. Smitten by one of the foreign dancers, Billy found a way to sit in on saxophone with the steel drummers while the troupe practiced their routine, which allowed him a validated introduction to the prettiest girl that he ever saw. None of the friends saw Billy for those entire two weeks, as he did his best to spend every spare moment that he could with the exotic exchange student. When the two blissful weeks ended, Billy felt depressed for months, even though the two young instant lovers promised to see each other again after graduating high school. If it were meant to be, then a few years in-between shouldn't affect their forever, they both agreed.

Her name was Paige, and she was all that Billy would talk about. By the time that particular summer hit, he had earned the nickname 'Lover-Boy'. Even though his new label embarrassed Billy, it didn't stop him from writing a letter to Paige almost every day for a year, and leaving the frog pond early to eagerly wait by his mailbox for her equally frequent love letters.

The communication between the long-distance love hopefuls slowed down during senior year, but the day after graduation, Billy sent Paige a letter, congratulating her for graduating, too. It included his phone number in case Paige wanted to catch-up by voice. A few days later, Billy received a call from Paige, at which time she invited Billy to visit her on the island.

Excited to see her again, Billy utilized most of the money that he received as graduation gifts, and booked a flight and hotel room. Carrying one suitcase and his saxophone, Billy boarded a plane for the Caribbean island a week later.

As the jet descended for its landing at the St. Thomas airport, Billy looked out through the small window near his seat and marveled at the blue-green color of the water below. Soon, there was lush land beneath him, and the palm trees got larger and taller as the plane quickly dropped altitude and landed on the island's short runway. The jet engines made a loud noise as they reversed direction for a quick stop. Billy felt the pressure of his seatbelt against his waist until the plane's momentum stabilized. Once he was allowed to unclick it, he thought to himself that nothing was holding him back. High school was behind him and he was eager to begin the next chapter of his life, beginning with that impromptu vacation to visit with the subject of his heart's obsession.

Billy couldn't take his eyes off Paige, as she maneuvered her car around hairpin curves that took them higher and higher above the remains of Blackbeard's castle and the terra cotta rooflines of Charlotte Amalie, the island's capital city. Once at the hotel, Billy and Paige sat at the resort's pool area, which overlooked the magnificent port below. Three cruise ships were docked near a marketplace of Caribbean rum, jewelry, and island cuisine.

Billy thought to himself that it was the hottest day that he ever felt in his life, while perched high on the island's hillside looking at the most beautiful place he ever saw. He couldn't tell if the floral fragrance that pleased his sense of smell was coming from the nature around him, or a perfume that Paige might have been wearing. All he knew was that the frog pond never smelled like that. An hour of catching up passed by in what felt like five minutes to both of them. Paige left Billy at the resort to freshen up, and headed home to do the same.

Later that night, a round vase containing freshly cut island flowers and a floating candle adorned the tabletop that the two reunited friends were sitting at. Tiki-torches illuminated the periphery of the outdoor seating area of the restaurant, allowing just the right amount of light for them to re-memorize the structure of each other's face, in case another few years would go by after Billy's vacation ended. As they held hands, they played an impromptu game of 'Twenty Questions' while waiting for their server to return with the tropical drinks that they ordered.

"So, what's your favorite color?" Paige asked.

"That depends on what the color is attached to," Billy answered, adding, "Right now, as I look at you, my favorite color is the blue of your eyes. It would still be my favorite color if the sea was exactly the color of your eyes, but it wouldn't be my favorite color on a house, you know? Ok, who was the first boy that you kissed, and when?"

"Like, a serious kiss? That would've been a couple of years ago. He was a cute, saxophone-playing hunk named Billy," Paige answered, while giving a wink.

The restaurant's server returned to the table with their drinks. While she was taking their food order, a jeep went speeding by, riding up on the curb and getting dangerously close to where Billy and Paige were sitting. Everyone seated in the outside area paused for a moment, followed by a murmuring. Billy and Paige finished placing their food order, and then resumed their conversation.

The sounds of chirping, buzzing, and peeping, seemed to hit Billy's ears from every direction. "Is the restaurant playing these sounds through speakers, or something, to make it sound tropical?" he asked.

"No, silly. You are *in* the tropics right now, listening to nature."

Just then, a tree frog leaped onto Billy's shirt, startling him and causing him to jump back in his seat. Paige let out a chuckle before asking Billy if he was afraid of frogs.

"Are you kidding me? My friends and I grew up around a frog pond. The difference is that the frogs at our pond jumped away from us, not at us. It just surprised me," Billy explained, while gently grabbing hold of the island creature, and holding it in his hands. "What a cool-looking frog."

The sound of tires squealing made Billy and Paige look toward the winding street again. Skidding around the bend was the same jeep, traveling in the opposite direction.

"That guy is going to hurt himself, or somebody else," Billy commented.

Paige took Billy's hands again from across the table. "So, do you want to have children someday?" she asked, refocusing Billy's attention toward her eyes.

Once I'm married, and have a good, stable life, I'd love to have kids."

A few minutes later, the same jeep careened onto the sidewalk, coming within a couple of feet of Billy's chair.

"That's it!" Billy said, while jumping out of his seat in a nervous panic. "Someone from the restaurant needs to call the police on that jerk. He must be drunk or something."

"Ugh. They're going to throw him in jail again," Paige said, looking distraught.

"What?" Billy asked. "You know that person?"

"His name is Gary, and he is on probation after doing a few months in jail for domestic violence."

"Against who?"

"Against me," Paige answered. "Gary is a good person, but he has a bad temper. We used to date," she explained.

"When did you two break up?"

"Yesterday."

"YESTERDAY?"

"I'm sorry, Billy, but I didn't want to lose the opportunity of seeing you again, had I told you that I had a boyfriend."

"But, *yesterday*, Paige?" Billy persisted.

"I know. I waited until the last minute because I was afraid of his violent nature. I actually slept over at a friend's house last night so he couldn't find me."

"Well, I suppose that I'm at risk myself, now."

"I'm so sorry, Billy."

"How could you have dated someone like that? You are such a gentle person."

"Gary wasn't right for me. I knew that, but I settled for him because of the lack of guys my age that live year-round on the island. Otherwise, it's a new group of tourists or sailors that pass through for a week, and then they're gone. I'm not a one-night-stand type of girl. I need to know that there's a tomorrow."

"But yet, you broke up with him for me, who will also be here for one week."

"I'm hoping that it'll turn into more than one week, if I'm to be honest with you, Billy."

Billy took her into his arms and kissed her forehead, while glancing once more toward the street. "Come on, let's see if they have any tables available inside."

Over dinner, Paige explained some of the brutalities of Gary's anger that left marks on her body. She lifted one of her sleeves to show Billy a bruise on her arm from his assault on her a few days earlier. He had hurt her after she worked later than usual, and his inaccurate thoughts about her whereabouts sent Gary spiraling into a jealous rage.

Frogs, Friends, & Funerals

Hearing of all the domestic violence that Paige had endured crushed Billy. He felt hopeless, but knew that he needed to find a way to protect her from that sort of abuse.

"So, on a happier note, my cousin is getting married tomorrow afternoon, and I'm hoping that you'll want to be my date," Paige said, while dropping Billy off, back at his hotel.

"I'd love to, but I didn't bring any formal clothes with me."

"You can borrow one of my brother's suits. He was a young businessman on the island, so there are several to choose from. You appear to be around the same size, and he had great taste, so if you don't mind I'll pick out one for you to wear."

"Where is the wedding being held?"

"Right here, at the hotel's restaurant. This is why I recommended that you stayed here," Paige explained, before leaning over to give Billy a goodnight kiss.

The next morning, Billy woke up and went straight to the hotel's front office and asked to make a private call to an off-island location. The front desk clerk offered Billy an unoccupied office, and Billy dialed Hank's phone number.

"Hello?" Hank answered.

"Hank, it's me."

"Billy! How's paradise?"

"It's absolutely beautiful here, but listen. If anything were to happen to me while I'm away, make sure to give the St. Thomas Police the name 'Gary' as a person to investigate. I don't have much more information on him yet other than he lives here year-round, but he recently got out of jail, so the cops could start there."

"Wait! What?" Hank said, with confusion and concern coming through the phone clearly within those two words.

"I don't want to panic you. I just want to make sure that someone from back home had at least a name, just in case."

"Billy, what is going on?"

"As it turns out, Paige had a violent boyfriend, who she only broke up with the day before I arrived."

"Seriously?"

"Yes, and I'm unsure what he looks like, so I don't know who I need to watch out for. This should make for an interesting week."

"Why don't you cut your trip short and head back home, then?"

"Because, I really love Paige, and besides not wanting to leave her because I can't get enough of her, I feel that once I fly home, he will harm her, or do even worse."

"Look, Billy, I am supposed to teach a pitching clinic at baseball camp this week, but I can postpone it and fly down so you can have some backup protection. You could still hang out with

Paige, and I'll just kind of hang out, off to the side somewhere."

"You would do that for me, Hank?"

"I owe you one, and even if I didn't, I'd be there for you, Billy. Let me look into flights so I can arrive by tomorrow."

"You're the best, Hank! The room next to mine seems to be vacant at the moment. I'll book that for you. Also, I'll be going to a wedding later today, so call the number that I'll give to you and tell the hotel clerk your flight info. I'll take the complimentary shuttle and will meet you at the airport. Pack light clothes because it is hot here!"

Paige arrived at the hotel around noon. She peeked into the restaurant to see how it was decorated for the wedding, while she waited for Billy to get dressed in the suit that she brought for him to wear. She was listening to the band sound-check when Billy walked into the room and stood next to her.

"Look how sharp and handsome you look!" Paige said, while her eyes watered.

Billy gave her a kiss, and then looked over toward the bandstand as they finished their sound-check in the cavernous, empty room. Appreciating their talent, Billy applauded for the musicians.

The steel-drum player jumped down from the stage and walked toward them. "You look beautiful, Paige," he said. "Is your cousin excited or nervous about her wedding?"

"I spoke with her this morning, and I think that she's a little of both," Paige replied, chuckling. "This is my friend, Billy."

The steel drummer extended his hand to shake Billy's. "Wait! Aren't you the saxophone player that we jammed with at that school on the mainland?"

"That's me," Billy answered, shaking the steel drummer's hand.

"Man, you were awesome! Too bad you don't have your sax with you. I'd have you sit in with the band today."

"Actually, Billy does have his instrument with him! He's staying here at the hotel," Paige said, excitedly.

A few hours later, the wedding was in full swing, and Billy was fitting in well with the band. The dance floor was packed as Billy exchanged solos with the lead guitarist throughout crowd-pleasing dance numbers. Aside from a few slow songs that he danced to with Paige, and the moment that Paige caught the traditional Bride's throwing of the bouquet of flowers, Billy spent most of the time performing with the band.

Paige had asked the hostess to keep Billy's dinner warm until he finished playing. While he was eating it at the end of the wedding, the band approached him and asked if he would have any interest in joining their band. Billy promised to give them an answer within a few days.

"You played so well. My brother would have loved to hear you on the sax," Paige said, while she and Billy walked among the well-manicured grounds of the hotel. "You know, they are the best band on the island. They are always busy, and you'd make a great wage playing for them."

"I feel bad that I was on the stage for most of the wedding. I didn't even get to meet your brother, and thank him for loaning me his suit."

"He wasn't there, but I felt like he was represented. He was really close to my cousin, and he would have loved to have been there."

"Oh, is he traveling for work, or something? I'd like to meet him at some point."

Paige took Billy's hand, changed direction, and started walking toward her car. "Come on, I want to take you for a drive."

Fifteen minutes later, Paige pulled into a small cemetery on the outskirts of town. Billy thought to himself that it was like no cemetery he had seen before. Less than half the size of the super market parking lot back home, it looked like a parking lot for the dead. There were rows of stacked cement boxes, and very few spaces for a living person to park a car while visiting. Billy looked over at Paige, as she turned off her vehicle.

"I suppose that it's time for you to meet my brother," Paige said, while opening her car door and stepping outside. Billy walked faster than normal to catch up to her. "He's right over here," she added.

Billy took Paige's hand and remained silent at first, as they stopped and looked at three cement boxes stacked in front of them. A quick read of the names and dates etched into the sides of the boxes allowed Billy to surmise that Paige's brother's body must have been laid to rest inside the middle one.

"I'm so sorry, Paige," Billy said. "You never mentioned having a brother in any of your letters to me."

"If I had mentioned my brother, I would have had to tell you about his death, which happened soon after you and I met. I didn't want you to feel any pity for me while we were getting to know each other."

"He was so young. How did he die?"

"He was very depressed and turned to drugs to cope. Unfortunately, he overdosed one afternoon," Paige explained, pausing before adding, "I found him hunched over the kitchen table when I got home from school."

"How sad, Paige," Billy responded, letting go of her hand and exchanging it for a hug.

"I was numb to it for a while, but I'm working through the reality of it. I keep this chair near the vaults. It's the one that he was sitting on when he died. Prior to then, it was the chair that my mother always sat on. Now I sit on it, sometimes for hours, and just read out loud to them."

"Them?"

"The vault on the ground is my mother's. She passed away just about a year before my brother died, which is what sent him off the deep end. They were extremely close."

"Wow, Paige, I had no idea. Is the top vault your father?"

"No, that's my uncle. He was the father of the bride at today's wedding. He was so hoping to walk his daughter down the aisle, but cancer won that race, just like it did against my mother who wanted nothing more than enough days to see my graduation."

"What about your father?"

"I never knew him. He was a sailor who just up and left on my mother. It's just me now."

Holding her as completely as he could, Billy whispered the words, "I love you, Paige."

Early afternoon, the next day, Billy met Hank at the airport. He was relieved to have some backup, or just an extra set of eyes to watch for Paige's ex-boyfriend, or to at least be a witness if anything were to happen because of him.

"Man, you are right. It is *hot* here," Hank said, while getting into the car.

"It is supposedly hotter than normal, I've been told," Billy said. "Even the natives are complaining about the heat."

"It was nice of Paige to lend you her car to pick me up. I thought that you weren't going to tell her that I was flying in."

"She spent last night at the hotel with me and I dropped her off at her work this morning. After thinking about it, I decided not to keep your visit a secret. That would have resulted in me needing to tell lies throughout your visit, and I want to be able to look back at my life someday and be able to say that I never deceived Paige," Billy explained, as he merged onto the main road from the airport lot.

"Look back on your life with Paige? It sounds like you two have quickly gotten very serious with your relationship," Hank said, hoping for some details.

"It's like something out of my control. I agree that things are moving quickly, but I can't help it," Billy explained. "I am in love with her, and can't imagine being with anyone else."

"Wait. Are you thinking about staying here on the island?"

Billy hesitated in giving an answer while he flicked on the car's turn signal and negotiated through a crossroad in the street.

"Like, what about college? You're already registered at the music conservatory for this fall," Hank continued.

Billy remained silent as he pulled into the cemetery where Paige's family was entombed.

"On a full scholarship," Hank added, before realizing that Billy had parked the car in a cemetery. He turned his head to look out of every window of the vehicle, and then asked, "What are we doing here?"

Taking the keys out of the ignition, Billy turned to Hank and broke his silence. "Since middle-school, what have I always said my life's plan would be?"

"Go to music school, make a living playing saxophone, then retire to a tropical island and give back by teaching music there," Hank recited, by memory.

"Exactly. Who is to say that I need to do those things in that order? I was offered a job playing sax for the top band on the island, so I'll be making a decent living right off the bat."

"You never mentioned a woman in your life's plan, come to think of it," Hank responded.

"You're right. I guess I just assumed that a woman would enter the scene at some point along the way. It just so happened to happen right at the beginning, apparently."

"But, are you sure, Billy? I just want to make sure that you thought this out enough."

"Follow me," Billy said, as he grabbed his saxophone from the back seat. He led Hank down a path lined with casket vaults, stopping at the three that held Paige's family members.

"Aside from a cousin and an aunt, who are still alive, we are standing at the graves of Paige's entire family," Billy explained, pointing out each one, individually, "That's her mother, this middle one is her brother, and the top one is her uncle."

"This is how they stay? Above the ground?" Hank asked, with genuine curiosity.

"That's what I thought, too, when I first saw them. I do think it's kind of neat that they are right here. Paige told me that she comes by all the time and reads to them."

"It certainly is different," Hank responded, while trying to get a better look at each of the container's construction, and means of lid security so nobody could open them.

"Paige pointed out a song that I played at yesterday's wedding, telling me that it was her brother's favorite, so I'm going to play him a private rendition of it now before I drive us up to the hotel."

As Billy finished the song, Hank offered up a small round of applause. "I'll tell you, Billy, if anyone can move the dead with music, it's you. I still get chills every single time I hear you play."

"Thanks, Hank. Who knows? Maybe one day my mother and uncle will relocate down here. Mom had been complaining about winters over the past few years. Along with you, those two have always been my biggest music supporters, and if they were to pass away before me, I could come here every week and play for them."

"You know that my statement about you moving the dead with music was just a metaphor, right? Once a person dies, their souls are gone from here, and back to God."

"I do know that, Hank," Billy said, while looking back over at the cement vaults. "These people are gone, but I am here. I can't leave Paige. Not only do I love her, but I care about her the same way that I care about our gang of friends."

Hank put an arm over Billy's shoulder, and as they both looked at the vaults, he said, "I love you, Billy."

Later that night, Hank dined with Billy and Paige at the hotel's outdoor restaurant. For several hours, while looking out over the twinkling of island lights below and the reflection of the moon on the Caribbean Sea, Billy and Hank shared stories of the frog pond, and quizzed Paige about growing up on a tropical island. By midnight, Hank felt like he gained a new friend in Paige, and was more comfortable with the idea of Billy staying to live on the island with her.

The next morning, Hank took Paige up on her offer to drop him off at Magens Bay on her way to work so he could get in an early run on the beach, before the sunbathers would arrive. He took note of the fragrant air of the new day as he walked onto the sand, passing a man who was emptying a weathered pickup truck to restock a fruit stand. The high tropical hills that surrounded the turquoise water gave the bay the shape of a heart. With the sun still too low in the morning sky to clear the hills, Hank appreciated the temperate air while he stretched his body for the run, and looked in every direction possible in an attempt to absorb the most beautiful beach he ever saw. Eventually, he set off running along the water's edge, but turned around after a dozen or so steps and jogged over to the man with the fruit. Hank explained to him how he would usually hold a weighted baseball in each hand when he went jogging back home, and asked if any of his fruit would mimic that. The best the man could do was to sell him two medium sized coconuts, about the size of softballs. Holding the two coconuts, Hank headed back to the shoreline. Invigorated by the setting in which he ran, Hank felt like he could have gone on for several more hours, but after many back and forth laps on the beach, he caught the first island shuttle of the day and headed back to the hotel. Paige was at work, and Hank wanted to have some one-on-one time with Billy, sensing that such moments would be rare once he flew home.

Meanwhile, back at the hotel, Billy was woken-up by a knock at his door. Figuring it was Hank returning from his morning run, Billy opened the door to find a stranger standing in front of him.

"Are you Billy?" the stranger asked, abrasively. "Is Paige in there?"

Realizing at that point that the stranger must have been Paige's ex-boyfriend, Gary, Billy became nervous and closed the door behind him and stepped out onto the narrow walkway between his and Hank's rooms.

"Yes, I'm Billy," he said, loudly, hoping that Hank might have already been back in his room and would have possibly heard him, so he could've been Billy's back-up that he flew down there to be.

Gary got noticeably irritated and backed Billy against a railing. Just below the railing was the outdoor restaurant's corrugated metal roof that slanted down and extended past the edge of the restaurant's high deck, with a thirty-five foot drop to a vegetation-covered hillside below that.

"I asked if Paige was in there! Someone told me that they saw her car parked here on the street this morning, so don't lie to me!" Gary screamed, poking at Billy's chest with two fingers.

"She's not here. She left a few hours ago for work," Billy blurted out, in a panic.

"That's it!" Gary shouted, while grabbing Billy's throat and choking him. "You're a dead man!" he yelled, keeping his grip on his neck.

Billy gave a few kicks in desperation, as he couldn't breathe or scream. While thinking that he had mere seconds left of life, Billy saw the sun peek over the distant hill. It forced him to squint just before hearing a loud thud, and feeling Gary's hands loosening from his neck. Billy frantically coughed and gasped for air, involuntarily, as his perpetrator fell to the ground.

A voice shouted, "Billy, I'm here!" It was Hank, who heard a voice scream out 'You're a dead man' as he stepped off the island shuttle. Hank had instantly darted up steps and walkways until he saw his friend being choked fifty or so feet away. Without hesitation, he threw one of the coconuts at the culprit, which hit him in the back of the head, knocking him out cold.

Hank checked Gary for a pulse, and once he detected one, left him on the ground and tended to Billy. It took several minutes for Billy to reclaim his breath and use of his vocal cords. Once he could speak again, Billy thanked Hank for saving his life, and asked him to help drag Gary into his hotel room.

"Don't you think we should call the police?" Hank asked.

"If we do, he'll end up back in jail, temporarily. This is something that needs to be dealt with for a long-term solution, considering this may be home for me for a while," Billy said, with a scratchy voice.

"What kind of a long term solution are you suggesting?" Hank asked, as he pulled Gary into

Billy's room by his shoulders, while Billy held his legs.

"I want to talk to him when he wakes up," Billy said, while placing a pillow under his attacker's head. "Would you mind getting some ice for me from the front lobby?"

Gary was slowly regaining consciousness when Hank returned with the ice. Billy met Hank at the door and asked if he'd mind waiting outside.

Moaning softly, Gary slowly moved his arm, and his hand reached up and touched the back of his head.

"Here, put this against where it hurts," Billy said, handing him a towel packed with ice.

Wincing his eyes to get a look at Billy as he tried to figure out what happened, Gary accepted the gesture and held the ice to his head. Neither of the two young men spoke a word for several minutes.

Keeping a watchful eye on Gary, Billy stepped into the bathroom to fill the in-room coffee maker with water to begin the brewing process. He picked up a few scattered articles of clothing from the floor and made a small pile of them in a corner of the hotel room, and then turned the desk chair around so it faced Garry on the floor, and he sat down and waited.

Eventually, Gary remembered just enough of what had happened to understand that he was in big trouble. He said nothing while he skirted himself away from Billy and sat up against the wall.

"I know about your violent past," Billy began. "Let me start by saying that if I learn that you touch Paige, ever again, chances are you won't wake up from what would happen to you."

Gary adjusted the ice that he held against his head.

"I also happen to know that if I make one simple phone call right now, you will be in jail by noon," Billy continued, while standing up and pacing short steps back and forth in front of Gary. "Paige told me that you're a good man with a bad man's temper. If that is true, then your behavior is something that you can seek help for. I get that it hurts to lose someone that you care deeply for, but the truth of the matter is that your physical abuse of Paige is the opposite behavior of someone who cares and loves. You now need to understand that you lost her by your own actions, and you must seek help for those actions. That is a promise that you need to make here and now, or I'm making a phone call."

Still confused on how Billy was almost unconscious from suffocation one minute, yet the next minute he was towering over him as the victor, Gary tried to find a more comfortable position for the ice against his head.

"You have one minute to make your decision," Billy warned. "Either the cops are picking you up, or you're calling a friend to pick you up."

Gary switched arms to allow the blood to flow back to his cold and numb fingers, and finally replied. "Look, I'm really sorry for what I've done to you just now, and for every time I've hurt Paige. I know that I have issues, but don't know how or where to get help. And, I don't have any friends I can call to pick me up."

"What about the person that told you that Paige's car was here?"

"He's just an acquaintance. I don't have any real friends."

"Not one?"

"My temper, I guess."

"Well, I don't have any friends on the island, either, but I'll be here for a while. Maybe we can learn to be friends, and I can help you find a place to get some help. I'd be sort-of like your sponsor."

"You'd do that for me?"

"It sure beats jail, right?" Billy said, offering his hand to pull Gary up from the floor. "Relax on the bed and I'll pour a cup of coffee and call a cab for you."

On the last day of his visit, Hank treated Billy to a chartered cruise around the island on a catamaran. As the vessel skimmed along the top of the gentle waves, the two friends reclined on oversized hammocks that dangled over the

Caribbean water and colorful tropical fish, reflecting on the unexpected twists of the week, and of their lives, so far.

"I can picture myself visiting you and Paige often, Billy. What a beautiful place to live, and an equally beautiful person that God has brought into your life, or you into her's," Hank said, as the catamaran captain walked over and handed each of them a hollowed-out coconut filled with a frozen smoothie concoction, made with native fruits of the island.

Billy reached over with his drink in hand, and clinked the side of Hank's frozen beverage. "Cheers to that, Hank, and visit anytime you want to." Billy looked at the coconut in his hand and added, "Especially when I need someone to save my life!"

Hank held up the coconut in his hand and said, "You know, it's kind of funny that the most important pitch I ever threw wasn't even a baseball, but a coconut."

"Ha Ha! You've pitched plenty of things besides baseballs, though," Billy reminded. "Do you remember pitching that chocolate cookie at Mr. Drummel's white pants?"

"Yes! I'll never forget that day," Hank reminisced. "I'm sure that Benny won't, either!"

CHAPTER 5

Benny

That first day of spring during the eighth grade of school wasn't Benny's favorite day, even though he won Rock Paper Scissors. Before the gang would head down the path of Benny's choice, he tried to initiate the countdown to do the frog wake-up shout, even though Hank wasn't there. Hank had a dental appointment after school and wouldn't get to the frog pond for at least another hour. Jenny, who was sitting on a huge stump doing homework, didn't mind the wait, nor did Terry, who was tutoring her. Charlie had made a quick dash toward the field with hopes of catching a glimpse of an aircraft he could hear flying overhead, so was in no rush to do the shout. Billy walked the edge of the pond, quietly scouting out any tadpole activity for his chance to earn that year's bragging rights of finding the first one. Grant stood there and became quite upset with Benny, who just wanted to get it done so they could use as much of what was left of daylight to get on with his choice of adventure.

Grant had appeared to be bothered by something at school over the few weeks prior, but it was odd that he carried it into the woods with him on the first day of frog pond season. "What is wrong with you?" Grant asked Benny. "We stacked hands years ago that we wouldn't do the shout without all of us being present. Do you know nothing about vows?"

"Relax, Grant. Like you said, that was years ago. We're getting older and things can change. What's the big deal?" Benny answered, trying to minimize his exposed disloyalty.

"You sound like my father," Grant said, under his breath.

"What did you say?"

"Nothing."

"No, go ahead and tell me," Benny insisted.

"It's none of your business. Besides, here comes Hank now, you cheater."

After the ceremonial shout, Billy claimed first tadpole sighting, to nobody's surprise.

"Let's re-do Rock Paper Scissors, now that Hank is here," Grant suggested.

"No way! We stacked hands on the frog wake-up shout, not Rock Paper Scissors," argued Benny, who had already started down his path of choice. Even though nobody had any money, Benny led the gang to the supermarket, anyway. It was getting late in the afternoon, so Benny didn't hesitate to jump into the dumpster on the side of the building while the rest of the friends remained at the edge of the path, several feet away. "Jackpot!" he shouted, while tossing packages of chocolate and marshmallow cookies over the top, toward the path entrance.

Hank and Billy ran out of the path and gathered up the packages while Benny climbed out of the dumpster.

"These are my favorite," Terry said, while opening one of the packages.

"Wait. Check the expiration date first," warned Jenny.

"We're good!" Benny declared. "They only expired yesterday!"

After devouring several cookies, Hank held one in his hand and wondered how far and accurate he could throw the expired round food. He aimed for one of the loading dock signs that were bolted to the side of the building, and he let it sail. Splat! An explosion of marshmallow and chocolate left a mark a few inches away from his intended target, entrancing the others to do the same. Within minutes, there were a countless number of cookie marks riddling the side of the building.

When they were almost out of cookies to throw, Benny was urged to dive back into the dumpster to collect more of them. Just after he jumped into it, Mr. Drummel, the store's manager, walked out onto the loading dock, heading for the dumpster with two large bags in his hands. Hank realized that Benny was going to get caught, so he took one of the remaining cookies, wound up like he would on a baseball pitcher's mound, and pitched it fast at Mr. Drummel in effort to distract him away from the dumpster. It hit him square in the rear end. The chocolate mark it made on his white pants made it appear that the grocer had a bathroom accident.

Hank's intended plan didn't quite work out, as an unaware Benny lofted packages of cookies out from the dumpster while an angered Mr. Drummel looked down on him from the loading dock. The manager's rage intensified when he looked at the side of his building to see that it was covered in chocolate and marshmallow.

Benny took a hit for the team and spent the next week washing the entire side of the building by hand after school. Mr. Drummel was so impressed with Benny's work ethic that he offered him a paying job of washing the loading dock twice per week, which Benny did for years. Eventually, he was promoted to work at the deli counter when he was a senior, and upon graduation, Mr. Drummel offered him a full scholarship to learn about food business management at the local college. It was the same college that Hank got a baseball scholarship to.

Benny and Hank remained close to each other throughout the college years, and for several that would follow. Entering adulthood with such close proximity to each other found them being each other's life-coach, counselor, champion, and consoler. Hank even asked Benny to be his best man when he got married. As a matter of fact, few friendships ran as deep as the one between the two. In addition, Hank credited Benny for saving his life from a watery ending, and not just once, but twice.

One winter day, during the holiday break of their sophomore year of high school, the gang of friends was gathered outside in front of the supermarket, waiting for Benny to get out of work. Coming from a path of the woods on the opposite side of the supermarket was a familiar set of kids from school. They were well known because they were the ones who were constantly being called to the principal's office because of something that they were in trouble for, and one of them had already spent time at a correctional school for fighting Hank, and pulling a knife.

After some small talk, they challenged the gang to a competition on the pond's ice near a tree-fort that they called their hideout. Nobody was interested in taking them up on their challenge, and by the time Benny walked out of the supermarket, the infamous group of kids was jeering them. Jenny suggested that they just walk away, but when they started making fun of Hank's baseball abilities, and calling him a scared jock, Hank got angry and agreed to their little challenge, speaking unelected on behalf of his group of friends.

Begrudgingly, the gang of friends followed Hank, who followed the notorious group into woodland that they weren't all that familiar with. None of them had walked through there more than twice in their lives, if at all. Even though the forest began just on the other side of the supermarket's parking lot, it very well could have been on the other side of the country to the gang.

The one who appeared to be the leader of their pack puffed away on a cigarette, while the kid walking directly in front of him slashed away with a hockey stick at the leafless vegetation that was resting dormant along the floor of the forest for the winter. Soon, all of the kids were standing in the middle of the pond, on top of the ice.

"Ok, one person at a time from each team will jump up and down five times. Whoever's foot goes through the ice first loses," their leader explained, while stepping up to be the first contender of his side.

Hank was chosen to be the first one to jump up and down for his side, with every one of his friends reminding him that he was the one who agreed to the challenge. Everyone stood in a large circle away from the two, as they counted to three and did their first jump.

"I don't think the ice is safe enough for this game," Hank said, with real concern. "Maybe we should postpone this for another week so the pond has more time to freeze."

All of the opposing gang began to laugh and mock Hank, calling him a chicken.

Hank's face reddened, and he initiated a three-count himself for the next jump. Upon landing, not only did his foot break through the ice, but also his entire body, which disappeared into the cold water below the ice.

"HANK!" Jenny screamed.

Benny forced the hockey stick out of the troublemaker's hands. He instructed Jenny to run to the supermarket as fast as she could so Mr. Drummel could call an ambulance, and he laid himself on top of the ice near the hole that Hank's body made. After a quick assessment of which way the water below was moving, Benny gently moved the hockey stick in that direction until it poked Hank, who grabbed hold of it.

"Grant and Billy! Grab my legs and pull me back! Hurry Up!" Benny shouted.

Once Hank's hands broke through the surface, Charlie reached down to grab his arm and assist with pulling him out. They quickly brought him to the side of the pond while the gang of derelicts ran the opposite way. Benny stripped Hank's cold and wet shirt from his body and wrapped him in Terry's blanket. Each of them huddled around Hank to create as much body heat for him as they could, while they listened desperately for the sound of an ambulance, and Benny prayed out loud.

Almost two decades later, Hank's wife invited Benny to join them and a few of her friends on a white water rafting excursion. Hank was glad that she invited Benny because she hardly ever wanted to do anything that included his friends. Their relationship was on the rocks, and Hank took the inclusion of his friend as a possible peace offering.

By then, Benny was the manager of the supermarket, accepting the position upon Mr. Drummel's retirement. His work hours were long, and he and Hank spent much less time together.

Hank looked forward to spending a day on the river with Benny. During the two-hour car ride getting there, the two friends caught up with each other, and reminisced about their childhood. They laughed over the raft that they made of branches and twine when they were kids. That was when they learned how shallow the frog pond was. On their maiden voyage, the twine started to loosen and unravel, causing the raft to break apart under them by the time they reached the middle of the pond. They both ended up in the water and realized that they could stand up and their heads would still be above the surface. It was also the moment that Benny learned how to swim, because he didn't want his feet to touch the muddy sludge below.

When they arrived at the rafting company's lodge, they were fitted with life vests and helmets. A short video showed them some safety measures, as well as introduced them to the lingo that their rafting guide would use while instructing new riders how to navigate their boat down the wildly turbulent river. Hank felt some uneasiness when forced to sign a waiver that took liability away from the rafting company if any unexpected injuries, or death, occurred. Having been athletic most of his life, Hank wouldn't have thought twice about signing the waiver in his more adventurous younger years. It wasn't so much getting closer to middle age that stripped him of his confidence, but rather his wife, who seemed to find pleasure in belittling Hank's natural skills, and eroding his ambitions.

Everyone joked about signing their lives away while they boarded an old school bus that was painted drab green. The vintage rickety vehicle creaked and swayed as it climbed the dirt road that took them higher up along the edge of a steep hill.

"Was the waiver for the raft ride on the rapids, or the bus ride to get there?" Benny joked.

"What's with all the boulders in that creek down there?" Hank asked the guide.

"That's where you'll be rafting. Those boulders, along with the rushing water, are what create the Class IV rapids. It's what you signed up for." The guide answered.

"What water?" Hank asked. "There's barely a trickle flowing down there."

The guide laughed to himself before answering. "There is a dam a mile or so up the river bed from here. There will be a controlled release of the water, and you'll be on the ride of your life."

Everyone took a look at the boulder-ridden riverbed below as the bus violently bounced and jolted its way along, forcing the riders to work at not bumping into each other while they became silent and more serious.

The rafting guide instructed the group to exit the bus and stand on the bank of the river before the water was released from the dam. Based on size and estimated weight, he arranged the order of where each person would sit in the large inflated raft. Hank was placed in the front row with one of his wife's friends that he wasn't very fond of, and Benny sat directly behind him, next to Hank's wife. Before they knew it, the water began rushing and they were off on an intense ride.

From the rear of the raft came shouted instructions from the guide, who was strapped-in on its upper edge. "Right paddle! Left oars out!" He was seated higher than the others so he could see over their heads to read the river.

The inflatable rubber watercraft moved so quickly that the guide's instructions seemed to change before any of the riders could comprehend his last command over the loud rushing water. Some nervous laughter came from Hank's wife as the raft cascaded over a small waterfall drop. He quickly looked back to see that Benny placed a hand on his wife's bare leg, most-likely to keep balance while the raft bounced and water sprayed incessantly at their faces.

"High side!" the guide shouted. "House boulder! Lean in!"

Hank quickly returned his view toward the front of the boat to see that they were about to collide with a huge rock. He braced for impact by grabbing onto the roping that was looped along the upper periphery of the raft. Upon contact, the boat bounced back and the inertia sent Hank flipping over the edge and into the rushing water. He hadn't noticed that his head hit the rock, which gave him a gash near his right eye. All he knew was that if he let go of the rope, he would either drown in the powerful rapids, or break several bones at a minimum.

His water shoes were instantly stripped from his feet, and he could feel his bathing trunks slip from his waist to his knees while he struggled to get his head above the rushing water long enough to gasp for a quick breath. Out of nowhere, two hands reached over and pulled Hank back into the boat by his life vest. Stunned, Hank pulled his shorts up and caught his breath. The guide steered the raft to the side of the river so they could regroup. His wife gushed about how strong Benny was, while the rafting guide placed a butterfly bandage on Hank's wound.

Once they got back to the lodge, Benny pulled a cooler from Hank's car, which was packed with various fruits and sliced turkey sandwiches from his supermarket, and distributed the food to everyone in the group. He gave Hank his sandwich last and took a seat next to him on the long picnic table bench.

"How's your head feeling?" Benny asked.

"I'm starting to get a headache," Hank answered, while unwrapping the cellophane from his turkey sandwich, before adding, "But it's my heart that I'm worried about."

Sensing that Hank was possibly speaking about his wife, Benny decided not to avoid the heartache comment, but twist it just enough to avoid the subject. "These turkey sandwiches just reminded me of the last Thanksgiving that we were all together for at the same time. I don't think that my heart has hurt any worse than it did that weekend."

CHAPTER 6

Grant

The Thanksgiving that Benny was thinking back to happened the year that they all graduated from high school. Everyone who went away to college came home for the holiday, and even Billy flew in from St. Thomas. All of the friends convened at Jenny's house late that afternoon for desert, which Benny provided from the supermarket.

"Before we eat this, did you get it from the store's bakery, or from the dumpster, Benny?" Hank joked, which got everyone laughing and talking about the frog pond years that began to feel more like a series of days than years to the young adult friends.

After desert, the gang of friends moved from the long dinner table to the living room, where a football game was being played on television. While they questioned each other about their changing lives, Barnaby made his way around the room, giving a nose rub to each of them, and accepting their pats on his head. The collie then stood at the sliding glass door that led out to the back deck and gave a weak whimper, alerting Jenny that he wanted to go outside.

"I don't know what's wrong with Barnaby," Jenny said, while sliding the door closed behind him. "I tried to give him some turkey earlier and he wouldn't take a single bite."

"Maybe he was just more excited about having you back home than he was about eating turkey," Charlie suggested. "I took him out into the field when I got into town yesterday, and he seemed fine, aside from not chasing after a squirrel that we saw like he would normally do."

"I don't know," Jenny responded. "He just seems different than he was before we all left town."

"Maybe Benny and I can come by more often and take Barnaby out for walks so he feels less of a void," Hank suggested.

"Oh, that would be great, Hank," Jenny agreed.

Barnaby never returned to the back door of Jenny's house that night. The next morning, Jenny's father led the friends on a search of the forest. The chill of the morning reminded most of them of following Jenny's dad on their very first hike to the frog pond. Barnaby was just a puppy then, and it seemed like yesterday to everyone. When they arrived at the frog pond, Jenny's father suggested that they spread throughout the forest by each taking a path. Terry agreed to stay at the frog pond in case Barnaby were to show up there. Jenny's dad gave Terry a whistle and instructed that whoever might find Barnaby should return to the frog pond to let Terry know so he could blow the whistle to alert the others that the search was over.

Terry was feeling weaker than normal that day, due to traveling home from college and a hectic holiday of making the rounds. He sat bundled on the large stump near the pond and waited. Soon, a noticeable wind blew through the trees, forcing some late autumn leaves to give up their grip and flutter down toward the ground. Terry watched as they disappeared behind the shallow ravine where Barnaby would always lay on hot summer afternoons.

Hesitantly, Terry jumped down from the stump and followed the falling leaves. When he arrived at Barnaby's special place, his fear proved to be true. He placed his blanket over the faithful neighborhood dog and tried to blow the whistle, but he could only cry.

By late that afternoon, a grave was dug for Barnaby on that spot where he had spent much of his summer napping time, and where he chose to die. Everyone agreed that he deserved his own memorial service, and the friends gathered at the stage area once again, where they took turns getting up and sharing memories of Barnaby.

In an effort to lighten everyone's mood, Jenny's parents hosted an indoor barbeque before the friends went their own ways again. Grant seemed to be unable to shake his somber mood throughout the long weekend, and Hank noticed that he was like that even on Thanksgiving, before Barnaby had died. When the friends were saying their goodbyes at the end of the night, Hank offered to walk Grant back to his mother's house so they could talk.

While they made their way around the block, Hank tried to gain clues about Grant's demeanor. Grant seemed to focus on how things used to be, while walking by houses that had new inhabitants since their childhood. When they arrived at Grant's home, Hank saw that there was a moving company truck in the driveway.

"What's that all about?" Hank asked.

"Where do I begin?" Grant replied, taking a seat on the stone wall in front of the house. "During Thanksgiving dinner, my mother and father explained to me that they were getting a divorce."

"Really?"

"Actually, no. They informed me that they've been officially divorced since August. They told me that they would have done it earlier, but agreed to stay together until I graduated high school so it would be easier on me."

"Gee, I'm so sorry, Grant."

"It just feels very surreal. I'm not shocked that they got divorced. They had been arguing constantly for years," Grant said, and then paused for a second to look at the moving company's truck. "Like, the next time I come home, this won't be my home."

"So, both of your parents are moving?"

"Yup, and a realtor is putting the house up for sale this week."

"Wow, Grant. That's a real bummer," Hank paused, and added, "I guess the only good thing is that you'll have two options of homes to go to the next time."

"How is that a good thing?"

"I'm sorry, Grant," Hank said again. "I guess I'm just trying to help offer whatever glimmer of hope I can. If there was a lot of fighting going on, maybe it will be a blessing in the long run."

"I'm not really thrilled about needing to visit two different places to see my one set of parents, though."

"True, but if you put things into perspective, you still do get to visit both your mother and your father. Billy hasn't had a father to visit for most of his life."

"I guess you're right. It's just that I've always pictured things a certain way," Grant admitted.

"I think that we've entered an era in our lives where things will be changing a lot more often than before. I do believe the key to a successful future is being able to cope with the changes, or at least finding ways to be accepting of the things that might not work out exactly how we may have envisioned them to, no matter how hard we try."

Hank was right. Grant wasn't very good at accepting changes in anything. He was very methodical in both his thoughts and his actions, and was often bothered when others weren't, especially if it affected him directly. Hank did have to hand it to him, though, the way he would carefully study each day's schedule thoroughly, including the schedules of other people or entities that he would be interacting with. For instance, there was the pre-planned, double-header day that Grant exchanged two of his Rock Paper Scissors wins for.

That morning, he led them to the library where the media room was going to be showing a movie about an oversized ape that had escaped and was tormenting New York City. The film was supposed to be screened at ten o'clock in the morning, which would have given Grant and the gang plenty of time to make their way back through the woods, past the frog pond, to Grant's perch above the quarry where blasting was to happen at noon.

Barnaby relaxed on the library's lawn while the seven friends went inside and took their seats in front of the media room's movie screen. They had given themselves a few extra minutes before the movie was scheduled to start in case any of them needed to use the bathroom before they dimmed the lights. Grant was the only one out of the gang to wear a watch, and he got increasingly upset with each minute that went past ten o'clock, when the film was supposed to be shown.

Storming out of the room, Grant charged toward the front desk, demanding that they start the movie. The librarian's monotone voice ensured Grant that it would begin as soon as the family that they were waiting for had arrived. They had called the library to ask if they could hold the film for a few extra minutes because they were running late. Hearing that set Grant off on another quarrelsome tangent that lasted past that family's arrival, causing Grant himself to miss the first ten minutes of the free film.

While incessantly checking his watch, Grant urged the others to leave before the end of the movie so they could get to the quarry to feel the earth move, and to see the large chunks of rock as they fell away from the façade of the cliff.

"Shhhh," most of his friends responded, wanting to see what would happen to the gigantic ape, and the woman that it was carrying around in its hand.

When it finally ended, Grant insisted that everyone run to the quarry, but by the time they reached the frog pond, Terry was out of breath and needed to rest.

"Go on ahead of us," Jenny insisted. "Terry and I will walk and catch up to you there."

Terry and Jenny heard the blast and felt the ground shake, even though they had not yet arrived at Grant's special place. A baby bird fell from a nest and landed in a bush next to them.

"The poor thing," Jenny said, while scooping it up gently and holding its frail body in her hands. "I can't leave it here to die."

"WE can't leave it here to die," Terry said, and knowing Jenny's next move, he held out his blanket like a nest. Once the bird was placed into it, Terry got a second wind and took off running back toward the library, as did Jenny, followed by Barnaby, who was frightened by the blast.

Jenny checked two books out of the library on caring for newborn birds, and headed to her house with Terry and Barnaby. Her father constructed a simple outdoor enclosure for the tiny bird out of some netting and old two-by-fours that were tucked behind his shed, so Jenny could nurse the bird back to health before setting it free. She had considered it a blessing that the movie ran late, placing her and Terry at exactly the right time and place to find and care for the fragile life that fell from a tree in front of them.

Grant, on the other hand, was upset that his plans were skewed, without all of his friends participating throughout his envisioned double-header day. When Terry and Jenny never arrived at the quarry, he felt like they betrayed him. Grant had no knowledge of the bird incident, and he cursed the two of them as he stormed away from the others in a huff, without any plan or direction for the rest of the day, which put him into even further disarray.

As he meandered aimlessly through the forest, Grant came across a Boy Scout troop at the Nine Men's Misery hill. He slowed his pace and listened in at what the scoutmaster was telling his troop. Not recognizing any of the boys, he looked at the patches that were sewn onto one of their uniforms and read the name of a town from the other side of the state. At first, he felt a little territorial and internally uncomfortable that strangers were inside "his" woods, but as he thought more about it, he got an idea. Grant headed toward the frog pond with hopes of finding Hank there so he could get his input on the notion.

"I think I found a way to make some money," Grant told Hank, as they walked around the pond. "Between the eras of when the monks had their monastery here, and the Nine Men's Misery battle that happened a hundred years before the signing of the Declaration of Independence, there is enough history in these woods to attract people from all over the place. I was thinking that I could give tours, for like a buck or two a person," he enthusiastically explained. "What do you think?"

"You know these woods as well as anyone, so why not?" Hank replied, while picking up a flat round stone near his feet and skimming it across the top of the pond. "Five skips!"

Grant accepted the unspoken challenge and looked around his immediate area and also picked up a rock. He side-armed it, and the thin stone banked sharply to the left and was swallowed by the pond with barely a splash.

"Not even one?" Hank taunted.

"You win some, you lose some," Grant said, before refocusing, "Look, because you always have smart approaches to ideas, Hank, I'll give you ten percent if you help me get this off the ground."

"Sure!" Hank agreed. "First, we should brainstorm on how to best do that, and write down everything that we come up with."

After dinner that night, Grant went to Hank's house where they came up with ideas for Grant's new business. They decided that a flier should be designed that would give just enough information about the historic location to entice an individual or organization into taking the tour. Copies of it would be mailed out to scouting organizations, summer camps, and church groups. They talked about the various points of interest within the forest that should be included on the tour, and that interesting facts and stories about them needed to be researched, and then presented in an entertaining way.

The next day, some of the other friends became upset when they learned that Grant and Hank got together privately, to plan out a business without anyone else's involvement or consent.

"This forest is ALL of ours. Why should Grant get to make money giving tours when the rest of us know this place just as much as he does?" Billy argued. "And do we want more strangers in our woods?"

"I agree," Benny said. "It's not fair that one or two of us get to make a profit from our woods, and the rest of us don't."

"It's because I came up with the idea," Grant stated.

After some back and forth rebuttal and suggestions, the friends compromised on the idea that the others would enhance Grant's tours by being character actors at various stops along the way. A few of their parents volunteered to design some costumes so the kids could dress like monks, soldiers, and Native Americans.

By the end of that summer, Grant's small business was the town's biggest, albeit only, tourist attraction. Around that time, though, was also when some of the friends became resentful of the bargain that they had made with Grant, which gave them only five percent of his profits. By the next summer, Grant continued to provide the tours of the woods on his own. On the positive side, they all still remained the best of friends, as the others in the gang began to develop their own interests and skills.

When he wasn't giving tours, Grant spent much of his time sitting high above the quarry, studying its workflow, procedures, trucks, and the equipment used to excavate wealth from the side of the land. His hours of intense pondering paid off as he worked on his engineering degree in college, and beyond.

For his senior project in college, Grant designed a piece of excavating equipment that had the potential of extracting more rock from the earth, without blasting, and within a much shorter amount of time than any machine that was being used in the quarry industry. Upon his graduation, one of the leading machine builders offered Grant a million-dollar signing bonus for the use of his design, and for him to engineer for them.

Grant thought that the money he was earning was great, but he found that he was battling long bouts of depression since his graduation. After eleven years of employment, and a well-invested portfolio, Grant retired from the company and moved back to New England. By then, his father had passed away, and his mother had remarried and moved to Florida. He decided to have a modern and expansive house built on Martha's Vineyard, mostly because it was the setting used for his favorite movie of all time.

Grant's new home was made primarily of glass and stone, and was set at the end of a long driveway that was paved with crushed seashells. Across the road was the beach made famous by Grant's favorite film. He thought that he would feel an excitement and sense of accomplishment when he walked into the dwelling for the first time, but the truth was that he felt immense loneliness as his footsteps echoed inside the home's vast foyer entrance.

With Memorial Day Weekend, and the sun rising higher in the sky, came an increased schedule of steamships and ferryboats, bringing vacationers to the island from Cape Cod. Rental jeeps and mopeds filled the streets, quaint shops sold ice cream and t-shirts to an endless stream of tourists, and an uncountable number of colorful umbrellas, bikinis, swim trunks, and sand pails competed for space and attention along the trendy island's coast.

Grant stood alone inside his immense showcase of a house and realized that he had everything that he thought he ever wanted, except for one thing. Happiness. The depression he had felt while living in the Midwest had followed him, and intensified. He eventually decided to seek some psychiatric help, at which time the psychiatrist suggested to Grant that he go back to work for a sense of worth, and to socialize.

"Go back to work?" Grant dismissed. "I'm a Millionaire."

"And?" the psychiatrist responded.

Grant sat in the comfortable oversized chair, silently facing the doctor.

"Listen, at least find some time to spend with a very close friend," prescribed the shrink.

Grant decided to invite the entire frog pond gang to Martha's Vineyard for Labor Day Weekend at the end of summer. He sent a mailer out to each of them, summoning them to the island, all expenses paid. Responses initially trickled in with wording like, "Sounds great" and "Can't wait," but by late summer, the only one of them that could spend the long holiday weekend with Grant was Hank.

Standing in the pedestrian area of the massive seaport dock, Grant recognized Hank right away as the over-packed ferry approached. Hank was standing on the upper deck, and Grant laughed when he saw Hank jump in surprise when the ship's loud horn blasted. It was the first genuine laugh that had come out of him in months.

"Where's the wife?" Grant asked, giving Hank a hug as he stepped off the ship's rampway.

"She decided at the last minute to stay home. Said she wanted to give us some guy-time."

"That's cool of her."

"I guess. I'm not convinced that that's the reason for her not coming, but whatever," Hank said, sounding a bit defeated.

"Everything ok with you two?"

"I'm not sure, but I've got a feeling that time will tell," Hank answered, handing Grant his travel bag before sinking into his luxury sports car's passenger seat. "Sweet ride, Grant."

Finally, Grant was able to show off some of his wealth and extravagant things. He spent a minute or two in the parking lot to show Hank all of the latest bells and whistles that the six-figure automobile was adorned with. He smiled as if he was letting Hank in on something when he asked him to push a certain button on the dashboard. The roof extracted itself, telescoping into its own panels and tucking in behind the trunk. Grant continued to watch the look on Hank's face as his seat moved under him, automatically adjusting to his size and weight. Satisfied by Hank's reaction of amazement, Grant pulled a pair of sunglasses from his visor and drove onto the busy island road.

Riding along the outskirts of the island on the way to Grant's home, Hank asked about the colony of colorful gingerbread-style cottages that they passed by. Grant gave him a quick response about them being summer weekly rentals. Hoping to refocus Hank's attention back on his expensive car, Grant tried to entice him with some of the features on the vehicle's sound system, but his eyes remained focused beyond the car.

"I think I could live in one of those all year round," Hank said. "That's all a person really needs," he added, not thinking about how his words were almost exactly the opposite of Grant's opulence.

Grant turned onto the road that led to his house. For the first time since buying it, he questioned to himself if the exuberant price tag of the car was really worth it, as his friend's focus went back and forth between the God-given ocean on one side of the road, and the adorable cottages on the other.

When they arrived at the end of Grant's long driveway, Hank read the side of the long van parked there. "Vineyard Shark Movie Tours. Grant, is this your company? Are you giving tours? You never said anything about it."

"I wanted to wait until you got here. I need to change the name of it, though. I'm finding that people are more interested in seeing the island, itself, than seeing sites where the shark movie was filmed."

"I guess that everything has its day," Hank suggested. "That movie did come out decades ago."

"But it is such a classic," Grant insisted.

"It is, and many more classic movies have followed. There's an entirely new generation of movie viewers since then, maybe two."

"But it is *such* a classic."

"Look, I love the movie, too. It's just that time marched on, as much as we hate to admit it."

"Speaking of time marching, I've got a tour starting in forty-five minutes. Let's eat a quick bite and then you can ride along as a tourist."

"I *am* a tourist, and you made me a shark movie geek a long time ago!" Hank laughed.

Grant pulled his van into one of the rare open parking spaces in the Oak Bluffs section of the island. The space sat across the street from an arcade, and the oldest carousel in America.

Hank looked at, and read out loud the sign that was secured to a telephone pole, "Island Tours". It had a dozen or so people extending from it, including a couple wearing matching shark-fin hats, and awaiting the tour van. "This space must cost you a pretty penny," he said.

"It ain't cheap, but I split it with a few other people that give tours," Grant said. "My goal is to have them all work for me someday."

The first stop of the tour brought Hank and the others to the beach directly in front of Grant's large modern house. Pulling the van to the side of the road, Grant spoke into a hand-held receiver and explained that the beach was used for the scene in which a young boy was eaten by the shark, pointing to where on the beach his ripped and destroyed inflatable raft washed to shore. Some of the tourists took photos of the beach from the inside of the van, while an equal amount gazed out the other side of the van at Grant's lavish home. Hank wondered for a moment if the beach scene site was accurate, or slightly off so that Grant could park the van in just the right spot so that his ego could feed off the tourist's admiration of his house.

Grant drove his van slowly through Edgartown, the most visited town on the island. Once a major whaling port, it was incorporated in 1671. "Hey Hank," Grant said to his friend, who was sitting behind him as he drove the van. "Can you imagine that this town began five years before the massacre at Nine Men's Misery? From my childhood to adulthood, it's almost as if I'm locked in the 1670's."

"Yeah, and giving tours based on a movie from the 1970's," Hank responded. "You're a seventies child, regardless of the century!" he laughed, while gazing out through the van window.

The pristine condition the town seemed almost imaginary to Hank. Beech trees lined both sides of the street, evenly spaced along the brick sidewalks. The historic buildings varied between a few architectural designs, but were harmoniously uniform with white paint and black shutters. Varied colored front doors were what gave them individuality within their seemingly exclusive settlement. It all made for a most picturesque backdrop to the multitudes of color and liveliness that the throngs of vacationers added to the scene.

"Anything carved into these beech trees?" Hank asked Grant.

"No. This isn't the frog pond. The locals here would run anyone out of town and off the island within minutes of them touching these trees, or anything else they feel is part of their historical island utopia."

"What's going on up there?" Hank asked, pointing out through the windshield toward a group of people amassed up ahead.

"Ugh. The protesters are at it again," Grant answered, explaining, "They are protesting against global warming today, even though most of them will drive away from here in their gas guzzling SUVs. Last week, they protested in support of illegal immigration. Such hypocrites, considering they all have fences around their homes to keep people out of their yards, and do all they can to keep poor people from affording even a single day on the island."

"Then, why are they even out here?" Hank asked.

"They believe and do whatever the media tells them. You should know that better than anyone, being a marketer and owning your own business."

"But, you'd think that they'd think, even just a little, while their hypocrisy gets exposed by their own contradictions."

"That's the problem," Grant replied. "People don't seem to think for themselves anymore, and so many residents here seem unattached to reality."

Hank's mind began to wander as he compared Grant's exuberant reality to his more humble lifestyle back home. For more than a year, his marriage had been on the rocks, and he knew that if he got a divorce, it would be difficult for him and his wife to survive, financially. That unpleasant thought dissipated before it could send Hank into a silent internal panic, which had been happening fairly often, but not over financial reasons as much as it being over him wanting to preserve his marital vow.

"But, why are they gathered in front of that particular building?" Hank asked.

"That's the Edgartown Town Hall, which actually has nothing to do with making decisions pertaining to the subjects of their protests. It just looks good for the television cameras," Grant said to Hank, before taking hold of the hand-receiver and speaking to the tourists in the van. "Coming up on the right is the Edgartown Town Hall. This is where the scene was filmed in which the shark hunter scratched his fingernails across the shark drawing on the chalkboard." He inched the van around the protesters, trying to not give them any attention during the movie tour. "This corner building on the left was used as the hardware store in the movie, where the chief of police bought the supplies to make the signs that would announce that the beaches were closed to the public."

As he narrated, he held up laminated photos from the film of each particular spot so the tourists' memories could be evoked.

"Where did you learn to give such entertaining tours, Grant?" Hank joked, trying to joggle Grant's memories of getting his first tour company off the ground in their childhood forest.

"Don't worry," Grant reassured, "I'll never forget my roots. You were an incredible mentor."

Hank gave a pat on Grant's shoulder, giving him a feeling of emotional security, which was something that Grant hadn't felt in years. Smiling, even though he was stuck in traffic in the middle of a quaint intersection in town, Grant took the opportunity to point out a huge and ornate tree that was visible from the van.

"If you look down the street on your right, you'll see a massive pagoda tree, folks. In the movie, the chief walked by it in one scene, as locals and tourists alike have done for almost two hundred years. It was carried back from China in a flowerpot by a sea captain that lived in that large house behind it. Considered to be the oldest and largest of that species in the country today, the sea captain planted it in 1837 to show prestige from his worldly travels."

"Worldly is right," Hank said. "I wonder if his prestigious tree helped him to climb up to Heaven at the end of his life on earth."

"What do you mean?" Grant asked, unsure that he actually wanted to hear the answer.

"From what I've read in The Bible, it seems that the more prestige one has on earth, the harder it is to get into Heaven."

"Does that mean that a person shouldn't try to succeed in life?"

"Hardly. I think what matters is what a person does with their success. If it's just to show prestige, then they may be wasting the talents that God gave to them, which they could be using to advance God's work here in the world. I wonder how many people back in the sea captain's day didn't like him because of him flaunting things. You know, human nature would have most feeling envy of wealth and dislike of arrogance over an admiration of it all."

Traffic began to move again. Grant remained quiet as he took a left turn and drove the van past high-end clothing boutiques, gift shops, and art galleries. After improvising his tour-route because of bottleneck traffic, Grant pulled the van into a portside parking lot, and spoke into the hand-receiver. "If you look across the water, you'll see a car being ferried across the sound on a small flat barge. That is the same barge that was used in the scene where the mayor of the town bullied the chief of police into keeping the beaches open for the Fourth of July, and for the island's summer revenue."

Grant waited silently while the tourists took a few pictures as the mini barge pulled up to the dock, and the car drove away. Grant followed behind the car, allowing the port to shrink and then disappear altogether in his rearview mirror. The van climbed a street that took them by quaint properties with white picket fences, inviting garden archways, rose bushes, flowered trellises, and cobblestone walkways that led to the granite doorsteps of historic homes. Each house had plaques mounted to them with circa dates that went back a few hundred years. At the top of the street was the town library, a large white church with forty-foot tall columns in front of its large entrance doors, and a cemetery with weathered gravestones that Hank felt was on a plot of land too small in size for the amount of history surrounding it.

Pulling the van alongside a strip of grass near a large barn, Grant grabbed hold of the hand-receiver and continued his narration. "Here on the right of us is the boathouse that was utilized to house the twenty-five foot long mechanical shark when it wasn't being filmed. It was constantly breaking down or not working at all, rendering it completely useless for any scenes during the first several weeks of shooting," he explained. "They began filming in May, and the film was budgeted to be done shooting by late June, but the production actually ran until late September because of the shark's mechanical issues. As a result, the movie's budget more than doubled, and the shark didn't get any screen-time until toward the end of the movie, which ended up being a blessing in disguise. The anticipation of the shark, whose presence was announced by two ominous notes of music, prompted the fear and anxiety of each moviegoer to reach depths as deep as their own imagination would allow, without actually seeing the terrifying man-eating fish."

Hank looked at the large barn that was covered with faded wooden shingles, and he slipped into thought. For a moment in time, the shingles represented the scales of a fish on the oversized tank of a building, as it kept the smooth-skinned mechanical monster contained in its belly just long enough for the director to shoot the movie differently. As a result, it became engaging enough so that a generation's imagination kept going back for more and more bites, digesting and regurgitation their primal fears over and over again with each movie ticket that it purchased, making the film one of the biggest summer blockbusters of all time. He glanced back at the other riders on the tour, trying to get a sense if they were contemplating similar thoughts by reading their faces. The couple that was wearing shark-fin hats was giggling about something on one of their phones.

Grant inched his tour van out of Edgartown, allowing him to drive more fluidly through a rural section of the island, uninterrupted by summer traffic. Rolling hills allowed views of the Atlantic Ocean's blue horizon to bob up and down behind farms and private estates along the way. Pointing out a house, Grant explained that a humble small log cabin originally sat on the same spot, and that the film's director camped out there for the entire summer when they were making the movie.

A few miles later, Grant pulled the tour van into a cemetery, parking it near a boulder with a celebrity's last name chiseled into the side of it. He gave a brief description of the late-night T.V. comedian turned movie actor, and opened the van's side door in case anyone wanted to take a photo with the deceased star's gravestone. One couple stepped out of the van and watched a comedy sketch of the entertainer on their phone, while sitting on the boulder six feet above his buried body. A few others got out to stretch their legs, including Hank and Grant.

"It's weird," Grant began to explain, "I stop here because it's along the way, and the halfway point of the tour, but very few people seem all that interested, or even know who he was."

"Again, time is marching on," Hank suggested.

"But, he was one of the biggest stars of the seventies," Grant stated, trying one more time to fight the obvious.

"He sure was, Grant, but that was decades ago. Fame is fleeting, and very few celebrities remain relevant beyond their generation. As fans age and die, so do their heroes and legends," Hank offered. "And, that's the best case scenario for most deceased celebrities. Often times, something becomes exposed or discovered about famous people that strips away the public's adoration of them, including the one that is buried right here."

"Boy, you're full of cheerful conversation today," Grant said, sarcastically, before calling the couple back into the van.

A few minutes later, Grant parked the tour van in the parking lot of an old fashioned general store. He explained that it was the island's oldest retail business, dating back to 1858, and that there was a public restroom inside if anyone needed to use it.

Hank watched as every person on the tour exited the van and headed inside. "I guess everyone needs to use the can," he said.

Grant laughed, and responded, "This is always my most popular stop, but not because of the rest room. People love to consume things. Throw a price tag on anything and people swim to it like a fish to a worm."

"What is it that they sell here?" Hank asked.

"Nothing that anyone really needs, but they have lots of it," Grant replied. "Come on, you've got to check it out."

The floorboards of the store's front porch creaked under his feet as Hank stepped up and walked to the entrance door of the general store. "That alone is worth the price of admission," Hank declared. "Think of all the people that have walked across these planks over the past century and a half. These creaks speak and cry of years gone by. If only we could understand them."

Inside, the floors were just as old. The scent of coffee competed against that of freshly cut flowers that were for sale, and bundled in an old metal washtub with just enough water to keep them alive, which sat on the floor just off to the side of the counter and its antique cash-register. As Hank and Grant slowly walked along the aisles, inspecting the store's wares, Hank laughed and said, "General store is right." The shelves were stocked with everything from basic staples, to penny candies, toys, tools and hardware, beach attire, vases, novelty items, tea sets, post cards, fancy soaps, fudge, fridge magnets, hair rollers, antiques, trinkets, candles and books. Post Office boxes were built into one of the walls, and a few locals sat huddled in a far corner sharing stories and island gossip.

"I'd like to meet the buyer for this place," Grant joked, while walking back toward the van.

"Seriously," agreed Hank. "They've either got to be a genius, or a scatter-brain."

"Honestly, if they've kept good records, they must have so much historical data by now that it must just be a formula that they go by. Think about it. A hundred and fifty years to learn what sells and what doesn't. There are thousands of various items in that store right now. I'd bet that they went through a hundred thousand items over the years and whittled them down to what's there today."

"True. Aside from annual trends and fads that come and go, it may have been refined so much that being a buyer for this general store may be a boring job after all," Hank pondered.

"Or worse," Grant added. "If it becomes predictable enough, a computer program will take over that job."

Grant knew exactly what he was talking about, considering some of the machinery that he designed and engineered forced many quarry workers out their jobs.

Grant's tour rolled into the tiny fishing village called Menemsha. The van stopped on a small peninsula that was lined with seaside shacks, or more accurately, landside shacks, as they were built on pilings over the water with just one edge of them touching the land.

"Any one of these would be my dream home," Hank said, while inhaling the salty air.

"Hank, these are one-room shacks," Grant responded.

"So what? I can only be in one room at a time anyway. What more does a person really need?

"Where would you put all of your stuff?" Grant questioned.

"I don't know. Maybe into a storage unit? Then again, if stuff is sitting in storage for any length of time, would I really need to keep any of it?"

Grant gave him a look as if he was talking like a crazy person, and then picked up the hand-receiver. "Folks, this tiny village is where the shark hunter had his fishing shack. Although the one in the movie was actually built specifically for the film, and taken down once it played its role, you can see several examples of similar shacks on both sides of the peninsula. You will also notice

that the Coast Guard station is still in existence
down there at the end of the road. The shark
hunter's boat passed by it in the film as it headed
out to sea with the hunter, the chief of police, and
the somewhat arrogant oceanographer on board."
Grant held up a photo from the scene. A few of the
tourists snuck away to peek into shack windows
with hopes of seeing skeletal remains of a shark's
jaw hanging from the rafters.

The final stop of the tour took them to the
farthest point of the island. A lighthouse
positioned high on a hill beaconed the van to a
parking lot that was positioned above The
Atlantic. The deep blue ocean visibly surrounded
them on three sides, with one of those sides
forcing eyes to squint from the sun reflecting off
of its surface.

"Between where we are sitting right now, and
that lighthouse, is where the film crew
constructed a billboard for the movie," Grant
explained into the hand-receiver, while holding
up a picture of it. "You may remember that it was
a welcome sign for the island in the film, which
was vandalized by someone who painted a shark's
fin coming out of the water behind a woman on a
raft."

One of the tourists made a snide remark about
driving all the way to the end of the island just to
see where a billboard no longer existed. Grant
explained that the attraction at that particular

stop of the tour had less to do with the movie, and more to do with the beauty of the island that all visitors should see. He explained how a ten-minute walk down a path would take them to the colorful clay cliffs of Aquinnah, and the rocky, yet beautiful, rugged shoreline. After telling them that the van would be heading back to Oak Bluffs in thirty minutes, he set the tourists free to explore, with a warning for them not to take any of the clay from the cliffs back with them.

Once the tourists got several feet away from them, Hank said to Grant, "So, I see that you are still finding paths that lead to cliffs and rocks."

"Ha! I never thought about that, but I guess it's true."

"The irony is that you've studied and engaged in extracting raw materials from cliffs, and here you are warning others not to touch them," Hank added.

"This isn't my land. It belongs to The Wampanoag Tribe of Native Americans. It's considered to be a desecration of the land, and it's even illegal for people to bathe or relax in some of the clay pools that form at the bottom of the cliffs after a heavy rain or an over-aggressive high-tide."

"Is it really that big of an issue? Is everyone getting into pottery making or something?" Hank half joked.

"You wouldn't think that it would be, but I'll bet half of the people will come back with clay packed in their pockets. I find evidence of that all the time when I clean the van after a tour."

"But, what do they even do with it?"

"Some may keep some in a jar as a souvenir, but my guess is that most just ends up being tossed back to the ground somewhere else within a week."

"Then why take any?"

"Because they've been told not to. Human nature."

"Then why even tell them not to?"

"To cover my own butt in case I were to get pulled over by the police and someone in the van has some. I need to verbally tell the tourists that it's against the law."

When the two friends got back to Grant's house, they sat on the back deck and watched the setting sun turn the wispy clouds in the sky from a pale white to shades of pink and purple. Hank could see that Grant was deep in thought as he slowly toggled an empty beer bottle back and forth, in-between two fingers. Hank got up and took the empty bottle from his hand, saying that he'd grab them another round from inside the house. He paused at a trophy case that was built into the hallway that went from Grant's back door to his vast and modern kitchen. He was reading some of the many awards that were illuminated within the shelves' casings when he heard Grant walk in behind him.

"Wow, Grant. National Designer of the Year? Three years in a row? American Innovation in Engineering Award? I knew you were smart, but, just, wow!"

"Thanks, Hank, but what's it all amount to?"

"It appears that it amounted to quite a bit," Hank replied, while extracting two beers from the fridge. "I mean, look at your house, Grant. Your car." He opened both bottles and handed one to Grant without looking at him. His focus was on a large glass cylinder that sat on display in the middle of his dining room table. Hank walked over to it to get a better look. "Grant! Is this what I think it is? Did you steal clay from the Aquinnah Cliffs?"

When Grant didn't answer, Hank turned around to see his friend in tears.

He walked over to him and put an arm around his shoulder. "What's wrong, Grant?"

"I'm sorry," Grant responded. "I didn't want this to happen tonight." He sobbed again, while Hank patiently waited. "The truth is that I seem to break down almost every night."

"Over what?"

"I'm not sure. I've been working with a psychiatrist in trying to figure it out. I just feel so empty. I have nobody special in my life, and on the rare occasions when I've gone on dates, I couldn't stop wondering if they were with me because of my money."

"Come on, Grant, you know that you are worthy of being loved for all the right reasons, regardless if you are rich or poor. You're such an intelligent guy, and any lady would be blessed to have you."

"But, I'm not even sure that it's that causing me to break down all the time. Yes, I get lonely, but what keeps eating at me is the meaning of my existence. I mean, was I placed on this earth simply to design equipment to help an industry make more money while putting hard working people out of work?"

"Of course not, Grant," Hank reassured. "You've got a lot to offer and you're still relatively young. There is so much that you could do, and unlike most, you'd have the financial means to actually do it."

"But, do what?"

"Do you remember when we were young and had that backyard carnival at Terry's house?" Hank asked.

"Of course I do."

"Do you remember what you said that night when we were cleaning up?"

"That when we grew up, we would all pitch-in and start our own amusement park?"

"That's what we stacked hands on first," Hank stated, "But it's what you said right after that."

"I'm sorry Hank, Please remind me."

"You suggested that we would give at least ten percent of our profits to help the needy."

"Yes, I do remember saying that, now that you've mentioned it," Grant recalled.

"I'm just going to come out and say it, Grant. All of this wealth and material belongings are very impressive, but it's not you."

Grant remained silent.

"I mean, don't get mad at me, but the things that you said today while we talked on the tour sounded like you, but your words seemed contradictory to your current lifestyle."

"Like what?"

"Like, when you talked about the movie producer living in a primitive log cottage while filming the movie. You and I agreed during the drive that he would most-likely have had less creativity if he was surrounded by opulence and privilege-afforded distractions."

"Anything else?" Grant asked, with a tone and facial expression that expressed disapproval of his judgments.

"Please don't get upset, Grant," Hank pleaded. "I'm only telling you this because I believe it may be contributing to the way that you've been feeling."

"Whatever."

Hank just looked at his friend, silently.

"Go on," Grant insisted.

Hank hesitated, trying to read Grants appetite for the truth, or lack thereof it, before continuing without making a conclusion either way, "Ok, like, when we were at the general store and you were talking about how people are drawn to anything with a price tag, which tells me that you get it, even though you might be just as guilty, and with much higher numbers on the price tags that attract you."

"Well, if that's true, hopefully my shrink will help me to correct my issues," Grant said, dismissively.

"If you ask me, I'd say that you'd have a better chance of finding answers in a church than in a shrink's office," Hank suggested.

"I'm not sure that I'm ready to have some minister try to tell me how to run my life."

"But you're willing to have a high-paid shrink tell you exactly what you need to hear that'll make sure you'll be locked-in as a patient for a long time? And don't even get me started on the medication that you'd most likely be placed on when all else failed," Hank argued.

Grant began to weep again.

"Look, imagine if you started your own amusement park here on the island, with a percentage of your profits going to charity. I can picture you feeling a level of self-worth that you probably haven't felt in a long time."

"I think that it's too seasonal here for an amusement park to make enough money for year-round sustainability."

"It might be worth looking into. Think about it, each one of the gang could come out now and then to volunteer, allowing us to keep that hand-stacking promise that we made in Terry's back yard."

"I don't know. How's Terry doing, anyway?"

"Terry's not doing all that great. I was going to tell you. He's back in the hospital."

"Man, that's too bad. I'll have to get him out to the island once he gets out of there."

"Sadly, Terry's mother told me that he might not be going home this time," Hank revealed.

"Are you serious? Is there anything I could do for him? Any equipment I can buy that would allow him to go home?"

"His mother said that the best we could do for Terry now is to pray for him."

"Do the others know?" Grant asked, with concern.

"I'm not sure who knows yet," Hank answered, somberly, as reality sank deeper into his consciousness. "It's been less than a week since he landed back in the hospital. Thankfully, Charlie flew in two weeks ago and visited Terry at home. Terry was too weak to walk with him to the frog pond, but was able to go for a ride. Well, Charlie drove Terry right to the airport and took him for a flight over the frog pond and woods. He told me that Terry had tears in his eyes, but a smile on his face from ear to ear the entire flight. I'm not sure who got the greatest gift out of it, Terry or Charlie?"

CHAPTER 7

Charlie

Happy Birthday to you – Happy Birthday TO you
Happy Birthday Dear Charlie – Happy Birthday
to you

Charlie blew out the candles on the airplane-shaped cake in front of him, forcing his lips to make an 'O' shape just long enough to focus his breath toward the small flames before those lips retracted back into the biggest smile that Charlie's face had ever made. The frog pond gang of friends surrounded the table, waiting for their piece of fuselage, or wing. Charlie turned sixteen, but unlike his friends that all received driving lessons for their sixteenth birthdays, Charlie got flying lessons from his parents. He had been obsessed with the notion of flying for as long as he could remember, but it was the summer before that one that turned Charlie's thoughts of being a pilot into a full-blown mission.

That prior spring was drier than most, and the conditions were ripe for the gypsy moth caterpillar invasion that the area had been forewarned about that winter. The furry, leaf-eating crawlers infiltrated the forest around the frog pond by the thousands, or maybe by the millions. Early evidence of their presence appeared as off-white silky tents that they constructed high in tree branches throughout the woods, even before the leaves fully came out that year. Once the leaves started growing, so did the appetites of the devastating caterpillars.

By mid-June, the gang of friends wouldn't dare step into the forest without wearing baseball caps or fishing hats. The reason for that was the seemingly endless cycle of leaves going in one end of the caterpillars and coming out the other. The perpetual sound of the pests' chewing, and their droppings falling through the trees to the ground, made it sound like white noise on a badly tuned television to anyone walking through the forest. Wearing hats made the friends feel like they had at least some protection against the tiny black droppings that fell from above them like hail.

Mid-July seemed more like late autumn in the forest, as more than half of the leaves throughout the woods had been eaten, leaving many trees bare. The infestation was state-wide, and became the leading story on the evening news many nights, when experts would explain how devastating the long-term effects might be to as much as seventy-five percent of the trees in the region.

Even though the defoliation of the forest allowed Charlie a view of any aircraft flying above, no matter which path he was on, he much preferred running out into the field to see them as opposed to a summer without the canopy of green leaves overhead. The devastation got so bad by August that the governor ordered aerial spraying over the entire state to combat the problem. Residents were ordered to stay indoors on certain days when the crop-duster planes would be blanketing the region with pesticide chemicals to kill the caterpillars. The public was urged to garage their vehicles, or to at least cover them with a tarp, so the chemicals wouldn't ruin the paint on them.

On the day that spraying was to occur over the frog pond, all of the gang gathered at Charlie's house, which was built on the highest point of the neighborhood. Charlie's bedroom on the second floor gave them the best vantage point to watch the airplane spray their forest, with hopes that their woods got saved because of it. The friends accepted the idea of staying indoors on rainy days, but having to stay inside when the sun was beaming felt almost unbearable to them. They did all they could think of to keep themselves entertained. Jenny brought board games to play. Grant brought a comedy movie to watch, about an airliner flight gone bad. Terry sat upon his blanket and listened to Charlie give a show and tell of all his airplane models, explaining how crop-dusters worked, while Charlie's mother provided the gang with snacks and sandwiches. They had practiced the best way to stack themselves at Charlie's window so they would all have a view of the aircraft, and as soon as they heard a plane, they got into position.

The excitement and anticipation levels rose in all of them, but especially in Charlie, as the sound of prop engines grew louder. He wasn't sure that he would ever get to see a real crop-duster in action, but there he was waiting for one to fly right over his house. The noise level got so intense that he could hardly contain his elation, and then in an instant, not one plane, but three of them flew so close over Charlie's house that he was surprised that one of the plane's landing gear didn't hit the roof. Charlie snapped a couple of photos and all of the friends gasped in awe, while they watched the colorful dust rain down on everything in its path until the planes disappeared into the horizon, over the trees. Just like that, the excitement was over, but they were ordered to stay hunkered-down indoors for at least another two hours after the spraying had ended, and told to avoid wooded areas for the rest of that week.

Once the governor gave the all clear to resume normal activities, Charlie was the first to venture to the frog pond, eager to experience the woods again without the sound of munching caterpillars. What he found when he got there changed the course of his life. He grabbed one of the nets and buckets that the gang kept stashed behind the large stump, and began scooping out the dead frogs that were floating on the surface of the water, and gathering the stiff ones that were dehydrated on the land. By the time the others arrived at the pond that morning, he was in such a rage over what the chemicals had done to the frogs that he vowed to them that he was going to do something about it.

When school began again that September, Charlie requested a meeting with the chemistry teacher on the first day of school. Charlie had developed a love for photography over the summer, taking photos of flying aircraft, mostly, up until the day of the spraying. He showed the chemistry teacher photographic evidence of the damage and death that the pesticide caused, and pleaded with him to help him come up with a spray-friendly mixture of ingredients that would still be effective in getting rid of unwanted insects. It needed to be less harmful to animals and the environment. The teacher agreed to work with Charlie after school in the Chemistry Lab, twice per week, until they came up with a safer, yet just as effective product.

A year later, at age sixteen, he was fulfilling his dream of taking flying lessons. One day, while driving Charlie to his lesson at the local airport, Charlie's mother noticed Hank walking home from baseball practice, so she pulled over and offered Hank a ride home, after a stop at the airport. Hank agreed, and the next thing he knew, he was seated in the back seat of a four-person Cessna airplane, behind his friend who had the controls of the small aircraft in his hands.

Through his headset, Hank could hear the commands that the flight instructor was giving to Charlie. Each syllable between them made Hank feel more nervous than he had in months, or years, or ever.

"In the event of an engine failure, where would you try to glide the plane to for a landing?" the instructor asked.

Charlie looked down to the ground in every direction and answered, "I would head for that field to the right."

"Wrong," the instructor replied. "That's way too far to glide an airplane with a non-working engine. You would have to try to skim it across that lake up ahead."

Hank's head turned several times between the two potential landing points, wondering what the actual chances of a safe landing were at all, as he wiped his sweaty palms on his pant legs.

The instructor gave Charlie the next command, which sent Hank's nerves soaring straight through the stratosphere.

"Ok, Charlie," he said, "Now, I want you to climb straight up until the engine stalls."

Hank mustered up all the courage he could find in effort to thwart a potential panic attack. He had a silent fear of heights that kept him from climbing trees near the frog pond with the others, or sitting in the highest bleachers when attending his favorite baseball team's games, even if they were the only seats that weren't sold out yet. All at once, he was wishing that he declined the ride that Charlie's mother offered. Hank wanted nothing more at that moment than to be safely back on the ground. Instead, he was seated vertical, heading straight up into the sky with Charlie positioned in a pilot's seat above him as he forced the plane to climb in a manner that it wasn't designed for.

"Keep climbing," the instructor said. "We are close to stalling, so pay attention to the sound of the engine and the feel of the plane in case you face these conditions without an instructor next to you."

"Roger that," Charlie responded, without any detectable nervousness in his voice.

Hank didn't care that he was drenched in sweat at the point that the airplane stalled and went silent. He just wanted to live, and began to silently pray hard.

"Push the nose forward," the instructor commanded.

Charlie didn't hear him clearly, so he responded, "Repeat."

"PUSH THE NOSE FORWARD!" Hank screamed, just as the instructor took control of the aircraft, and then turned around to signal at Hank to remain quiet.

"Let's go over the maneuver again," the instructor suggested. "Remember, when the engine stalls, you are to push the nose of the airplane forward so it goes into a dive, forcing the propellers to spin and jumpstart the aircraft."

Charlie came up with an excuse to end the lesson early, in effort to preserve his friend's nervous system and state of mind. Once they landed, Hank felt a sense of relief like never before. Additionally, his level of respect for his friend Charlie hit higher altitudes.

During their senior year, Hank helped Charlie start an aerial photography company, and put together a marketing plan that allowed Charlie to introduce his business across the region. It grew to include crop-dusting that utilized Charlie's own organically based pesticide. As a result of Charlie's unique blend of environmentally friendly materials, made to protect many varieties of crops from damage-causing insects, Charlie's business expanded into other states. By the end of his second year in business, he was able to purchase his own crop-duster airplane so he wouldn't have to rent one anymore. Charlie eventually relocated to a rural area of New York State after falling in love with an apple farmer's daughter.

Fast forward several years to Charlie's wedding weekend, and Hank was being picked up by Charlie at the nearest train station to the apple orchard where the wedding was going to be held.

"What's the matter, Hank? Did I scare you out of flying all those years ago?" Charlie joked, as he gave his friend a hug and grabbed Hank's garment bag from his hand.

"Ha Ha!" Hank laughed. "No, I've flown quite a bit since then, but no flight has been more memorable than the one I took during your lesson. That's for sure!"

"I don't mind picking you up at all," Charlie said, while placing Hank's garment bag flat onto the bed of the apple orchard's pickup truck. "But, why didn't you drive your car, like you did when you came out here for that interview a few months ago?"

"I don't want to bore you with a long story," Hank responded, while stepping up to sit on the truck's passenger seat."

"I'm all ears. We've got just about a fifty-minute drive to the orchard."

As Charlie pulled away from the train station in the small college town on the Hudson River, Hank began to share with him some of his woes from the past year, which stemmed from his failed marriage.

"Look, it's your wedding weekend," Hank said. "I don't want to be a downer talking about my train-wreck of a marriage while you should be getting excited about yours."

"Ah, I see what you did there," Charlie responded. "Is that why you rode the rails to New York?"

Hank looked out the window as Charlie drove the pickup truck onto a high bridge that took them over the Hudson. "I wish that was the reason," Hank answered, sounding exhausted from life itself. "The truth is that during our divorce, she agreed to pay any and all taxes and penalties for any of the years that we were married, in exchange for her walking away with everything, including our business, financial assets, land, house and everything inside the house."

"What? Are you crazy or something? You conceded all of that?"

"That's what Jenny said, too, when I visited her in Savannah after the divorce. I guess that I just wanted that nightmare to be behind me, especially when she started telling anyone who would listen that I was a widow-chasing gold-digger."

"Man, that's like the opposite of the Hank that I know."

"That's what Jenny said, too," Hank recalled. "But, little good the divorce decree did, considering that the IRS doesn't recognize divorce decrees and still has me on the hook for the taxes, making me ineligible to re-register my car."

"How much has she paid-off so far?"

"Nothing. Zero. Zilch. She moved out of the state without paying a penny." Hank angrily explained.

"Ugh! Well I can tell you now that I never liked that woman." Charlie admitted.

"Again, those were Jenny's very words, too. Why didn't anyone warn me?" Hank asked. "Actually, you don't need to answer that because Jenny already did."

"Who's running the business if she skipped town?"

"I was told that she sold it, though I'm not sure how she was able to with the tax thing going on. I was also told that she already remarried, to someone with lots of money, and a few businesses of his own."

"I could have told you that *she* was the gold-digger. She only pressured you into marrying her because you were being courted by the major leagues to coach for one of their teams. From the conversations that you and I have had, it seemed apparent that she wanted out as soon as the baseball league hired a different coach."

"Yeah, go figure. That coach has already been replaced."

"So, how are you getting around?" Charlie asked, while taking his eyes off the road for a moment to mentally identify a small airplane that flew perpendicular over the pickup truck.

"I've been taking public transportation."

"You mean you ride the bus?"

"Bingo!"

"Are you serious? How long will you have to do that for?"

"Until I can get a date in tax court and get it resolved, which can take more than a year to get in, according to my lawyer."

"You need to ride the bus for an entire year? I sure hope that you have a good lawyer to bury that witch!"

"Considering my current state of poverty, I have a state-granted lawyer for free."

"They're always the ones that cost you the most in the long run," Charlie warned, as he turned the pickup onto the long rural road that led to the orchard, as well as past the farm where a famous music festival took place in the late 1960's. When they got close to the former festival site, Charlie asked, "Whatever became of your job interview to be the marketer for the festival site's owner? You'd be perfect for that job."

"Actually, it was to market a campground that the owner of what's left of the farm wants to build. The actual site was purchased by a business mogul who built an amphitheater on the land, next to the original field that is being left empty."

"I'm surprised that the businessman didn't put the music venue on the original site."

"He couldn't"

"Why? Land preservation?" Charlie guessed.

"That would be an honorable reason, but wrong. The reason is, most likely, that a venue on that very footprint would expose the hoax, and faux legend that it has become. That entire event was manufactured to kick-off a new movement, and era, based on chaos. There were slogans of peace and love on the surface, but with a lot of sinister intent lying patiently under the façade. The closer I got to marketing the remaining parcel of land, and the more I studied the original event and the people behind it, the less interested I became in promoting an entity that I believed was deceitful. I sure wasn't going to continue a lie that started at two-hundred thousand people in attendance, and then swelled out from the promoters' mouths to three-hundred thousand when they saw what they were getting away with, and ended up at a half-million people being the number of attendees as the decades passed. It's so ridiculous that they might as well say that there were a billion people at that concert. Have you seen the site?"

"Of course. I live here, and have seen it by land and by air," Charlie confirmed.

Then, you must realize by now that a fraction of the first number of people is closer to the actual attendance number, and that holding a single event on the very spot would prove it all to have been lies and propaganda. I mean, you could barely fit a football stadium on that footprint of land. Most stadiums hold sixty to eighty thousand people, and are designed to hold the maximum amount of attendees within that space of the stadium. Take a look of any photo of the original music festival and you'll see multitudes of blankets sprawled out, people laying around and lounging, and the farther away from the stage people got, the more spread out. I'm just not into spreading lies and false narratives."

"Sounds like you really did your homework. I can see how that would have triggered your decision not to work for anything or anyone connected to that," Charlie responded.

"Actually, that wasn't even the catalyst of my refusal. When I drove out here for the interview, the woman who owns the land of the proposed campground site took me for a walk through a field and some rugged woods where she wanted to build it. As I suggested ideas for it along the way, she shot them down as fast as they came out of my mouth, even though she had zero useable ideas of her own. She wanted to keep the terrain natural, and have vacationers set up tents among the brush on the forest floor, as they did during the original festival. She had no interest of listening to my concerns that anyone who went to the original concert would be too old to want to sleep on the ground, in a tent, if they were still alive to begin with. She didn't want to hear that anyone since that generation would expect simple amenities like running water and showers, neither of which she was planning on including."

"Yeah, I can see how that would be a tough business to market, hence your decision not to," Charlie said.

"As good of a reason that would've been to not work for her, it wasn't what ultimately made me say no." Hank continued to explain. "I knew for sure that I couldn't work for that woman when we were walking through the forest portion of her property and came across a pure white cat that seemed to be resting in between two branches of a tree, just above arm's length. It was facing out toward the debris-filled path, dead, and not fazing the woman at all. It looked like some sort of a sacrifice hanging there."

"That's creepy," Charlie said. "I'd be hesitant in wanting to work for her, too."

"And that's not even why I decided not to."

"There's more?"

"There sure is," Hank continued. "I tried to provoke her into addressing the dead white cat, and said that I wondered if animals go straight to Heaven when they die. Her response was that I must believe in fairytales if I believe in God. *That* is when I knew for certain that I couldn't work for her."

Charlie waited several seconds before responding, "You know, I'm not a believer in all of that either, Hank."

"That makes me sad, Charlie. Maybe you just haven't given it enough thought?" hoped Hank.

"Look, I did the whole church thing with my folks when I was younger. I'm just not buying it."

"Buying what, specifically?"

"A dude dies, hangs out in a grave for a few days and then heads up to Heaven? Why doesn't he come down and give an annual speech, or something?"

"I believe that if you open yourself up to God and pay attention, you can hear Him speak to you every day."

"I kind-of find it easier to believe that hundreds of thousands of people were at a music festival than one person going to Heaven after death."

"Wow, even with physical evidence that proves it would be impossible to fit that many people on that plot of land? People would have to be stacked on top of each other, three people high, without an inch of field to spare."

"Maybe we should talk about something else."

"Ok, but I'd bet that however many people were at the festival, most of them believe in God by now, as they near the end of their lives."

"Maybe so."

"I would think that you'd put some faith in God, and a life after death, considering the risk that you take by flying all the time."

Charlie remained silent.

"Do you think that Terry is just laying there in the ground, and that's it?"

"Hank, I just don't know."

"Well, I hope that you'll at least give God another chance. Maybe a different church, or just start reading The Bible."

Charlie continued driving, showing no emotion either way.

"Please, do me a favor and don't tell the others about me riding the public bus."

"Speaking of others, why didn't you just ride in with Benny? I think he's getting in tonight," Charlie asked.

"I haven't been able to figure Benny out lately. It's like I've got to beg him to get together. He seems to have a completely new set of friends over the past year, so it's not like he isn't hanging out, period. Just not with me. I mean, I had a monumental birthday over the past year, as we all did, and I had to plead with him to meet me at the frog pond to reminisce and have a few beers. He did show up, but stayed for just one beer, and appeared to be distracted by something on his phone the entire short time we were together. It would have felt awkward to ask him for a ride now. I'd hate to force him into a four-hour drive with someone that he no longer wants to hang out with, for some reason."

"That's strange. I wonder what gives?"

Later that day, most of Charlie's friends had arrived at the farm after dropping off their bags at the nearby motel. Charlie and his wife-to-be hosted a cocktail party around a huge bonfire in one of the orchard's pastures. Stories and laughter wafted up into the air with the bonfire smoke, as drinks flowed down and friends hugged and caught up with each other. Charlie did notice an oddness about Benny, and suggested to his future wife that the seating arrangements for the wedding dinner be changed so that Hank and Benny wouldn't be seated side by side.

The next morning was picture perfect, as a crew put the finishing touches on a large white tent positioned between two different varieties of apple groves. Green trees, dotted with red fruit, grew in rows upon gently flowing hills as far as the eye could see. The lifting morning fog revealed more of the orchard's beauty as the hours passed by. A white archway, adorned with daisies and heather, was set up under the sun, near the tent. Two sections of white folding chairs created a makeshift aisle in between them for the bride to walk down, and once the dew dried from the grass, a white cloth walkway was rolled onto it.

By 1pm, the wedding guests began to arrive as a rented harpist strummed her golden stringed instrument near the ceremony area. Well-dressed people clustered into small groups of familiarity, including Charlie's gang of friends, who made a circle just off the edge of the groom's side of seats. Jenny adjusted Hank's tie while Grant and Benny scanned the bride's side to see if any apparent single ladies were in attendance.

Dressed in a tropical shirt, white linen pants, and beige sandals, Billy grabbed a beer out of the ice from one of the well-stocked metal apple tubs near the orchard's barn. "Too soon?" he asked, as he joined his friends who were empty-handed.

"Still in island mode, Billy?" Benny asked.

"Nothing wrong with that," Hank declared, taking a light jab at the one friend that still lived nearby, but avoided him at all costs. "I think I'll have one, too," he added, before he turned around and headed for the tub of beer. "Who else wants one?"

Soon, each of the friends had a beer in their hands, but was forced to guzzle them down when they saw the minister arrive and the other guests take their seats. Benny let out a not-so-quiet belch and Hank quietly reprimanded him on the way to the seating area. Charlie came out from the farmhouse, dressed in a tuxedo, and headed straight for his friends. He gave them each a hug before he took his place near the minister. The harpist strummed louder, and everyone stood up as Charlie's bride came out of the house and headed down the aisle, dressed in a while-laced wedding gown that seemed to flow harmoniously with the mild breeze and angelic musical notes.

"She looks so beautiful," Jenny said softly.

"She looks hot," Benny responded, under his breath, which prompted a nudge into his ribs from Jenny's elbow.

"I think that the priest is a friend of theirs. He looks so young, though," Billy said.

"He's not a priest. He's a minister," Grant corrected. "He can get married. I think that's his wife over there."

"Wow. She's hot, too," Benny said, resulting in a harder blow to his ribs from Jenny.

"I'm surprised that he has a minister at all, considering that Charlie doesn't believe in God," Hank said, wishing immediately that he could have retracted his words.

"He doesn't?" Jenny and Billy responded at the same time.

"Welcome friends and family," the minister began. "We are gathered here today to witness the union of-"

"OUCH!" The bride screamed, while moving erratically in front of the guests. "OWW!" She screamed again, swatting at her dress and crying hysterically. "OWW! They are stinging me!"

Charlie took off his jacket and shouted out for the guests to turn their heads before quickly lifting his bride's dress above her head to release some bees that had flown under her wedding attire. He shouted out to his almost father-in-law to run into the house for some ice cubes, and Hank got up and made a dash for some closer ice from the tubs of beer near the barn.

"Get her Epi-Pen!" the bride's mother shouted to her husband who was running toward the house. "She's allergic to bees!" she added with a panicked voice.

"I'm monitoring her breathing and airway," Charlie shouted. "She's avoiding anything that may harm the-" Charlie stopped, realizing he might have said too much already.

"Harm the what?" Billy asked his nearby friends.

"Is she pregnant?" Jenny pondered quietly.

"Her body is too sexy to be pregnant," Benny said.

"That's enough, Benny," Grant said. "That's your friend's bride. What's wrong with you?"

Hank delivered to Charlie a sports jacket cradling as much ice as the makeshift sling could carry, and then returned to his friends. The minister announced that the bride and groom were going to take a half hour to regroup, and pointed out the tubs of complimentary beverages that Charlie's friends had already discovered.

By the time the ceremony finally concluded, each of Charlie's friends felt a bit of a glow from consuming a few beverages in the sun on empty stomachs. The guests congregated under the tent as they circled the tables in search of their names on place settings. Hank and Jenny found theirs and sat down. Billy found his and took his seat next to Benny.

"I don't think that's your seat," Benny said. "It says William."

"And?" Billy asked.

"And, you're Billy, last time I checked."

Billy looked at him sideways in amazement. "You're kidding, right?"

"About what?"

"You do realize that my real name is William, right?"

Benny just stared at him with his mouth agape.

"You seriously didn't know that Billy is a common nickname for William?"

"That makes no sense to me," Benny answered.

"What makes no sense is you knowing Billy his entire life, and somehow not ever knowing his real name," Hank said, from across the table.

"I guess we can't all be as smart as you, Mr. Bus-Rider," Benny said, just as Charlie rose to make a toast, and as Hank confirmed that he lost a friend.

"I decided to give the toast today in the absence of my friend, who couldn't be here to celebrate with us. His name was Terry, and he was supposed to be my best man. Whenever I was feeling down about not having anyone special in my life, he'd always tell me that my perfect mate was going to land right in front of me when I least expected it. He always encouraged me not to give up on the notion of eventually being yoked to my perfect person, at exactly the right time. Terry was wrong about one thing, because *I* was the one that flew in, and landed right here in New York, in front of the love of my life."

"CHEERS!"

All in attendance enjoyed the rest of Charlie's wedding day, and even though Hank and Benny avoided each other for most of it, all of the frog pond gang stacked hands and promised to reconvene somewhere within the next two years.

CHAPTER 8

Hank

The following years proved to be difficult ones for Hank. To put things into perspective, one needs to know Hank from his frog pond years on up, and nobody knew him better than his close group of childhood friends.

Ever since he was a young child, Hank could see the big picture of most situations like an adult would, and maybe even had a clearer picture than most of them. Certainly, his intents were more pure than most, and consistently evident in his actions. For example, Billy's grandfather was placed in a nursing home when Hank and the gang were in second grade together. Billy was sad because his grandfather was always at his house after school to get Billy off the bus while his mother was working several jobs as a single mother. They were very close to each other, but Parkinson's disease forced him into the nursing home so he could get twenty-four hour medical attention. As a result, Billy had to start going to the crabby lady's house next door after school until his mother got home, just before his bedtime. On the school bus, Billy would often explain to Hank how much he missed his grandfather, but expressed an even deeper sadness when he'd suggest that his grandpa was probably even more sad than him, having to be locked up in that home every day with hardly any visitors. It bothered Billy that his mother had to work so hard that they only got to visit him twice per month. Hearing that made Hank sad, too, so when the music teacher at school said that the Christmas Concert still needed someone to fill the voice of Santa Clause for the following week's performance at the nursing home, and that the class should do their best "Ho-Ho-Ho" to see which student was the best, Hank pulled Billy next to him. When the teacher gave the signal, students started to do their best Santa voice, with Hank digging extra deep and loud to make his voice sound like an adult. The teacher pointed toward Hank and Billy, asking who made the deep Santa tone. Hank held up Billy's arm, and then coached him over that weekend so that he could pull off the deep voice when he got to his grandfather's nursing home. Billy's performance was outstanding, and his proud grandfather introduced him to his roommates and nursing home neighbors. The school allowed Billy to spend the rest of the afternoon at the elderly home with his grandpa until his mother could pick him up after work. It was a special day for Billy, and one of the last days on earth for his grandfather, who passed away just a few weeks later.

One day during third grade, Hank's class was cleaning up after an art project while the teacher stepped out of the room for a moment. Grant tossed his pair of scissors over to the plastic bin that the teacher kept them in on top of the heater, but the scissors glanced off the side of the bin and slid out the open second-floor window. The class fink told the teacher that one of the boys threw a pair of scissors out the window. When the teacher became irate, asking whose parent she needed to call, Hank said that he was the one that tossed them out. He knew Grant's alcoholic father enough to know that Grant would receive a bad beating as soon as he got home. Hank thought it was the right thing to do, especially because the bruises all over Grant from his father's fist and belt hadn't even healed yet from the last beating. The teacher ordered Hank to go outside and retrieve the scissors in the rain. When he got out there, he looked under every window of that class, unsure which one Grant had accidentally thrown them out of. All Hank knew was that his teacher told him not to go back inside the school without them. In a panic, Hank started searching the entire parking lot, and when his teacher saw him a hundred or so feet away from the building, she screamed out the window for him to return to class. Meeting him at the top of the stairs, she grabbed Hank by an ear and dragged him away to the principal's office. Grant sat silently at his desk while some of his classmates laughed at Hank's demise.

During the month of May in their fifth-grade year, Jenny had caught a case of the chicken pox. Knowing that she would miss a few weeks of school, her teacher sent work home for Jenny to do, which Hank hand-delivered to her house. When he got there, Jenny's mother let Hank in, signaling that she'd be wrapping up her phone call in a minute. While he waited, Hank heard Jenny's mother tell the person on the other end of the phone that Jenny might have to go to summer school. She explained that with their recent week away on vacation, and then her unexpected chicken pox outbreak and resulting two more weeks out, she was at risk of failing the history class that she was already struggling in. Upon hearing that, Hank snuck away from Jenny's mother and headed down the hallway to Jenny's bedroom. He knew how contagious she was, but he wasn't going to have her miss half of summer, which included her first year playing for a Little League baseball team. He gave a quiet knock, and once he knew Jenny was awake, he opened her door and headed straight to her with a big long hug. Jenny asked him if he was crazy or something, and Hank explained how he was going to be her tutor so she could pass history class, and the fifth grade. For the next few weeks, Hank had Jenny copy every single word from several text book chapters by hand, explaining that she'd be able to recall the information better when it was time for her to take her final exam. It also allowed Jenny to have some company while her itchy chicken pox bumps faded away, just as Hank's were beginning to kick in. Jenny felt bad that Hank missed the first few weeks of baseball practice because of his longer bout with the pox, and she visited him every day to play an electronic game of baseball, being the only friend who already had chicken pox, therefore being immune.

Hank's anxiety level pertaining to heights hit a higher-level one-day after school in his eighth grade year. He was walking home after visiting the frog pond, passing Benny's house. Hank wondered why he was looking up and talking to the large maple tree in his front yard. Benny explained to Hank that he got mad at his little sister, and put her cat outside to punish her. It was the cat's first time out of the house ever, and Benny was freaking out because the cat wouldn't come down from the tree. His sister was crying, and it was the first time that his mother had trusted Benny to stay home alone after school, and get his sister off the bus. His parents were going to be home in an hour or so, and Benny had never climbed a tree before. Hank hadn't either, but he faced his fear of heights to help out his friend, who still needed to keep an eye on his sister. As he climbed higher, and got close to it, the cat got scared of Hank and scurried back down, running to Benny's front door. Benny let the cat in and yelled "thank you" up to Hank, telling him the cat was inside and that he could get down now. Unfortunately, Hank was scared to death and frozen from fear, high up in the tree. He pleaded with Benny to call the fire department to come get him down, but Benny kept saying that he'd get in trouble if he called them, and that Hank should muster up the guts to climb back down. An hour and a half later, when he saw his father's car coming up the street, Benny promised that he would explain the situation over dinner if Hank promised to remain quiet when his father got out of the car. Another hour passed, and Benny's family finally walked out of the house. Hank's arms and legs were so sore that he didn't know how much longer he could have taken the pain for. Instead of rescuing Hank like he thought they would, Benny and the rest of them got into the car to go somewhere. Hank began to scream out for help, and Benny's dad called the fire department to get him down from the tree. Benny got grounded for a week, and then wouldn't speak to Hank for another two weeks after that.

Hank was very protective of Terry throughout every grade of school, especially when anyone picked on him for being less athletic than other boys his age, or tried to ridicule him for being over-studious. To give an idea of the maturity of Hank's character, one needs only to look at the day when Terry lost the U.S. Air Force blanket that he carried with him everywhere. Terry was so distraught at the frog pond that morning that Hank decided to come up with an excuse for why he needed to go home for a few hours. When he got there, he took out some money from his lawn-cutting jar and hitchhiked into the city, which was three towns over. He was on a mission to buy Terry a new Air Force blanket from the Army

Navy Surplus Store. When he got home that afternoon, he placed the folded blanket in a large black garbage bag and headed into the woods to find the gang, and to surprise Terry with the replacement blanket. When he got close to where they were gathered, he could see that Terry had found his blanket, so he turned around and went home to store the new one under his bed, in case he ever lost his blanket for real. Terry never did misplace his blanket again, and Hank never told him of the day that he traveled halfway across the state to buy him a new one with his lawn-cutting profits.

During their sophomore year school trip to Washington D.C., Hank and Charlie were roommates in the hotel that their teachers reserved. During the first day of the trip, the students were separated into two groups to tour The White House and The Lincoln Memorial. Charlie found the hands-on experience interesting and informative as the tour guide gave facts while they were inside each building. Hank, who was with the other group of students, found his tours to be informative, too, but in a different hands-on sort of way. Charlie's high school girlfriend was part of Hank's tour, and he witnessed her holding another student's hand several times throughout the day. Hank's heart sank for Charlie, and he kept trying to figure out how to best break the news to him when they were back at the hotel. The pit in his stomach was almost unbearable as he prepared the words while Charlie headed to the snack machine in the hotel lobby. When Charlie returned to the room, Hank knew right away that Charlie had already found out, as he was drenched in tears after seeing her kiss the other boy in the hallway. Hank consoled Charlie the best he could, and once Charlie fell asleep, he wrote a letter to his teacher and slipped it under her hotel room door. His teacher found the letter to be so well written, that she agreed to his request for him and Charlie to go off-schedule and spend a day at the Air and Space Museum with one of the chaperones, instead of what was pre-planned. Even though it didn't take away Charlie's pain, it allowed his thoughts to be somewhat distracted by a love that nobody could take away from Charlie.

After high school, Hank attended the state college, with tuition fully covered by a baseball scholarship. Hank was the college's star pitcher, helping his team win three championships during his four-year tenure at the college. Having graduated at the top of his class, he had a decision to make. Either play for the regional minor league baseball team with hopes of hitting the majors, or accept a marketing management position with a prominent corporation that paid four times more than he would earn with the minor leagues. He opted to go the corporate route, and remain active in local baseball by coaching for the town's baseball league, where he got his start.

Hank became a local baseball legend, and the town even named a baseball field after Hank since taking four of his teams to the national championships over the years, which was a first in the country for any coach. He was invited to speak at a national coaches' conference in Philadelphia, which is where he met the woman that he would marry. Hank felt honored to accept his award, but wasn't one to attend such gala-type affairs, or else he might have recognized for himself that she chased whoever she thought would get the farthest in the industry. Trade magazines had just announced Hank being courted by the majors to coach one of their teams. Unaware of her tactics, he fell for her ill-intended seduction, hook, line and sinker.

Hank agreed to marry her a month later, after she convinced him that soul mates and fates have no set timeline. She explained how her former husband, a previous co-owner of a major league team, died unexpectedly, and that she never thought she'd want to get married again until she met Hank, who was unaware of her sexual advances to several men in the league as early as a week after his passing. They had a private ceremony in front of a judge, and she moved to

Hank's New England town where they bought a house together.

For the next year, Hank continued to work as a successful businessman while the major league went through their process of interviewing candidates and assessing their skill sets against the needs of the specific teams that were adding to their coaching rosters. Finally, he was informed that he didn't make the final cut, and if that wasn't enough of a letdown, the corporation that he was working for went through restructuring a month later and Hank lost his job. His wife showed signs of being more disappointed than Hank, and convinced him into starting their own business in town.

Hank took out a third of his retirement account to pay for the household bills, and his wife cashed-in one of her deceased husband's IRA's to get the business start-up funded. She set-up the business as a woman-owned company, telling Hank that it would be good in the long run for tax reasons, instead of having both of their names on it. Hank focused his efforts on the build-out of the interior of a strip mall space where the business would be, worked through the best operating procedures, and marketed the business. Benny had even swung by on several nights during the build-out phase to swing a hammer. Once open, Hank would spend many nights working after hours, some nights until three o'clock in the morning, to keep up with customer demands. At the end of the first year in business, Hank and his wife were able to confirm that it was a success, having brought in three hundred and fifty thousand dollars in sales. What that year also brought, though, were some shady behaviors by his wife that Hank couldn't put his finger on.

His wife scheduled a telephone call with a medium, who convinced Hank that he should head across the country to work at a baseball camp for a year, and that it would be good for his career, and that his marriage would be stronger because of it. When Hank got to the west coast, he found a marriage counselor that was willing to conduct sessions via telephone, as Hank had some terrible suspicions. At the end of the first session, the counselor informed Hank that he could tell that his wife had already checked-out of the marriage. Upon hearing that, Hank drove the three thousand miles back across the country to return home and work on things, face to face.

When Hank got back to New England, he realized that his wife had pushed him into heading out west so that she could have him be as far away as possible, while she did all she could to erase him from her life, while securing for herself all of the material things that they accumulated together. Hank found the locks of his house and business had been changed, his name taken off their shared bank account, as well as his health insurance cancelled. He spent the next six months sleeping in a cement basement shelter on an air mattress, while trying to understand why he was all of a sudden homeless, out of work, and headed toward divorce court.

Around town, Hank heard echoes of nasty, untrue rumors that his wife was spreading about him. To prove her wrong, Hank eventually agreed to give her everything - the land, business, house and all that was in and around it, in exchange for her paying the taxes that he suspected she had messed up, like the year previous. Everyone thought that he was a fool to accept such a bad deal, but Hank just wanted to silence her slanderous tongue. Reputation was very important to Hank, and the person who moved to Hank's town in marriage was ripping his name apart.

Hank was forced to cash in the remaining funds from his retirement account to pay for his terrible divorce lawyer, and to rent a small apartment. As his credit crashed in the wake of his divorce, Hank had to sell what he was able to keep of his baseball equipment, like pitching machines and batting cages. He even sold his prized baseball that was signed in the early 1900's by his favorite baseball player, so he could survive another month.

Within the first six months of his divorce, Hank applied to more than a hundred jobs, sending out his impressive resume but getting no offers. Eventually, when he followed up with some of the companies that he applied to, he was informed that he'd have a tough time finding employment with having such a low credit score. While Hank struggled, his ex-wife hired a manager to manage the business that Hank built and made successful, and moved to another state, where she opened a second business based on the first one's business model.

Hank eventually went to work as a salesperson for a large furniture store. With twenty-five to thirty salespeople on the floor at any given time, there were often more salespeople in the store than potential furniture buyers. With income being one hundred percent based on commission of furniture sales, Hanks eyes were opened-up to how selfish, devious, and backstabbing his co-workers, and humans in general, could be. In his mind, he compared the salesperson-to-customer ratio to being like a small oasis in the desert, with several animals surrounding it, but only enough water and food there for a few to survive. Hank was the last one to survive out of the dozen of the salespeople that were in his training class just ten months earlier. His survival on the sales floor wasn't based on his success in sales, but rather that he refused to be a quitter, as he continued to sell what was left of his personal belongings on the side to survive real life.

Refusing to steal customers away from other salespeople when they weren't looking, like they did to him, Hank was left at a disadvantage, resulting in him leaving work after twelve-hour shifts with zero dollars earned. Those salespeople who were picking Hank's pockets behind his back were telling him to 'hang in there' to his face. What felt the most torturous to Hank was walking past all of that expensive furniture for hours on end, knowing that it would take him years to afford another living room set, or even a single mattress, since his ex-wife had stripped every piece of furniture away from him.

Trying to remain as positive as he could, Hank would seek out the spiritual meaning for every stage of his life. He found that he could read the faces and body language of those who were entering the store, with many going through divorces or other personal tragedies themselves. When he sensed that they needed to talk, he would sit with them and lend an ear, sometimes for an hour or more. Hank would also give extra attention to the elderly when they arrived to look at lift-chairs, with the hopes of remaining in their homes for as long as they could before being forced into a nursing home. He sold very few lift-chairs because he knew that many of the customers that needed them were on a fixed budget, and Hank would quietly inform them of the furniture store down the street that sold the same units for less money.

As previously mentioned, Hank cared about his reputation, especially after years of treating others right, coaching and inspiring hundreds of young baseball players in town, being a successful businessman, and just generally doing all the right things throughout his life. Unfortunately, his pride hid him away from those who would have been most likely to purchase from Hank. Whenever he saw someone walk into the furniture store that he knew, he would disappear into an employee bathroom for as long a time as they were looking at furniture for their homes. The last thing that Hank wanted was for anyone to know that he was selling furniture after being so well-respected in town, never mind having to explain to anyone why. Additionally, he never wanted to put anyone in a position where they felt like they had to buy something just because they knew Hank.

The only time that he sold furniture to someone that he knew was when Benny came in and demanded that Hank sold him a coffee table set for his living room, using Hank's employee discount, with no commission paid to him. Hank would have done that for Benny, even without Benny's insisting on it. Hank found his friend's demanding demeanor to be repulsive, especially

when he accused Hank of selling him one less
end-table than he thought he paid for, upon the
delivery of Benny's order. Hank showed him the
invoice, which reflected everything that the table
set came with at that price that he paid, so Benny
could see that Hank not only didn't overcharge
him, but gave to him a better price than any other
customer ever paid for that same set of tables.
Benny ended up returning his furniture order to
the store, resulting in Hank having to pay for the
restocking fee himself.

Hank knew that he needed to get out of the
cutthroat furniture business to preserve his faith
in mankind. More job applications were filled out,
but the response rate being a silent zero was
deafening to Hank, whose spirit was growing
weary and discouraged. One day during his shift,
he was sitting on one of the showroom sofas that
were tucked away in a corner of the store. He felt
like he was on the verge of a breakdown so he
positioned himself as far away from coworkers
and customers as he could. Seemingly out of
nowhere, an elderly woman asked if she could rest
her legs by sitting on the sofa next to Hank.

For the following hour, Hank and the woman
chatted about life. Hank ended up opening up to
her, apologizing when tears started racing down
his face. The woman, who was a retired
schoolteacher, suggested that he consider being a
substitute teacher, where he could make a

difference in the world, and earn a few dollars for survival while doing it. Hank's boss eventually found him and the elderly lady talking to each other on the sofa, and abrasively told Hank that 'if the old lady isn't gonna buy, she needs to fly, or to you it's bye-bye'. Hank helped the elderly woman off the sofa, handed his nametag to the boss, escorted the woman outside to her car, and never returned to the furniture store.

Two weeks later, as a substitute teacher, Hank entered the elementary school that he attended with the frog pond gang. Being a male teacher when females predominantly held that role, Hank was embraced by faculty and students alike. Hank's reputation of being a great teacher spread throughout his town's school system, as well as those from the neighboring towns. Before he knew it, he was teaching at mostly every school throughout three different towns. The meager pay that substitutes made kept Hank struggling, financially, but deep down inside his soul felt rich. Students would surround him in the halls with cheers whenever he'd arrive at a school for that particular day.

One day, when Hank was just starting to accept where he was in life, he received a phone call that would shake him to the core. The voice on the other end of the line was Hank's ex-wife's new ex-husband. Their marriage lasted just over a year, and he felt that he needed to reach out to

Hank regarding some secrets that had been exposed during the short-lived marriage. He began by explaining how she had convinced him to sell his house to pay off her bills because both of her businesses had failed. A week after his house sold, she asked for a divorce, changed the locks, and blocked him from any communication with her. Hank shared similar stories with him, saying that he was still dealing with the disastrous aftermath from the evil woman. The new ex-husband said that he had information for Hank that would change the way he looked at certain others, particularly the one who was the best man at Hank's wedding to the repugnant woman, and the wedding photographer, too. When Hank told him that he was prepared to hear whatever he was to be told, the new ex-husband shared information and evidence that Benny was having an affair with her behind Hank's back, before and after she moved away from Hank's hometown.

Hank was crushed, and he called Benny right away to hear what he had to say about it. Benny outright denied it. Hank suggested that his behavior and elusiveness to their friendship would make sense, if tied to an affair, and that he was going to call the new ex-husband back for more details and additional evidence. By the next morning, and three back and forth calls later, Benny finally admitted to the charges, and the two stopped talking to each other, completely. Hank was devastated, but not because he still had feelings for his ex-wife. He didn't. He was blown away that one of his closest friends on earth had betrayed him that badly.

Hank was so distraught over what he had learned that he needed to share the news with at least one of his other friends from the gang. To his uttermost amazement, Jenny was so surprised that she didn't believe him, and then, nor did Billy, or Grant. Charlie believed him, but blew it off as having already passed, suggesting Hank should move on. Hank felt very alone from that moment on.

In a daze, Hank continued his life as a substitute teacher, trying to hang onto whatever semblance of his life seemed to be worth anything at all. When his car registration was about to expire, Hank went to the state's automobile registry department to renew it. He was denied, due to taxes owed for past years. When Hank dug into it, he learned that his ex-wife never paid the taxes, as per their divorce decree, and that the Internal Revenue Service still considered him liable for the taxes, as they wouldn't recognize divorce decrees. They informed Hank that thirty thousand dollars would be needed from him if he ever wanted to register a car in the state again. Hank was shocked and angry. The Internal Revenue Service said that his ex-wife was less affected because she moved out of the state, so there was nothing that they could penalize her with.

Hank spent the following weekend walking through the frog pond woods alone, trying to figure out where his life was heading, considering his means of transportation was stripped away from him. His anger had him throwing buckets of baseballs at photos of Benny and his ex that he taped to a tree, which may have evoked a series of the most powerful and accurate fastballs that he ever threw. He was so exhausted by that Sunday night, both mentally and physically, that Hank rested his head on top of his pillow and prayed to God, asking for a way out of the nightmare that he found himself in.

That next Monday, Hank called in sick and used the day to call the public transportation company so he could understand how the bus system worked, where he could buy tickets, what the schedules were, and which schools that he taught at were close enough to the bus routes for him to still teach at.

The next morning, Hank wore a coat that was too heavy for the season, and he headed to the nearest bus stop. He wore that coat every day because it had a large hood on it that he could hide his identity under. Hank kept his back to the street to minimize being spotted by the people in town, such as students, kids he coached on the baseball field, their parents, and also Benny. Even with his hood on, he felt uncomfortably exposed as he stood at the edge of the street under sun, snow, and rain. He welcomed stormy weather because it gave him an excuse to wear his hood, knowing how silly he looked while wearing it on sunny days, which he did anyway.

Hank kept to himself when he first started to ride the bus. He tried to assess everyone's situation while he studied the faces of riders from all walks of life. Had he rode the bus a few years earlier, before his life took such a drastic turn outside of his control, he would have most likely judged them unfavorably. Even so, he quickly made a determination that he didn't want to eventually have the physical appearance of some of them. Hank's lack of health insurance had already resulted in some of his back teeth being broken, even though he brushed and flossed them more than anyone he knew. A smile from a rider across the aisle gave Hank a view of something he feared, which was a mouth with very few front teeth. Hank didn't know whether to feel bad for the person, or disgusted by the lack of care. What he did know was that the person may have had a similar story, that Hank had no knowledge of, so he needed to detain any judgments he may have made at a more judgmental point in his life. He also thought about how few would put that much thought into it, and how they might jump to the most unsavory conclusion about that other human being, within seconds.

It made Hank sad and concerned, knowing how the general public would be judging him the same way as soon as they saw him getting on or off the bus, even with all of his visible teeth still in place. One thing he did make a judgment on, though, was that not a single person on the bus showed any evidence of being successful, at least not by worldly standards, or even the barest of social expectations.

During the seventh month of Hank riding the bus, a woman got on and sat on one of the seats that faced sideways, which were reserved for the elderly. Hank kept looking at her, as he was certain that he knew her from somewhere. Eventually, she tugged on the cable near her seat that alerted the bus driver to let a passenger off at the next bus stop. Hank watched as the woman slowly got off the bus, with help from her dull-pewter metal cane. It reminded him of the elderly couple that he and Jenny met on the trolley tour bus in Savannah, but he still couldn't figure out how he may have known her. The elderly woman stood on the sidewalk, looking back and forth, noticeably confused as to where she was supposed to be going. Hank quickly got up as the bus pulled away and asked the driver to stop again so he could get off, too.

Hank walked over to the woman and suggested that they sit on the bus stop bench for a moment so they could, together, figure out her intended destination. While they sat there, the woman explained that she knew where she was going, but had forgotten how to get there. Hank asked a few additional questions, which allowed him to figure out that she was going to a health clinic, which was four additional bus stops down the road. While they waited for another bus to arrive, Hank and the woman began to chat, and she realized that she had met Hank in the past. It was on the sofa that was tucked away in a corner of the furniture store.

Hank felt relieved that the mystery of who the woman was got solved, but he also felt sad to see the woman riding on the bus instead of driving her own car like she had on that day when they met. The woman explained that her driver's license was taken away from her after she hit a fire hydrant with her car when passing out while driving. She said that the bus was her only transportation option to get to her appointments at the free medical clinic. There was nobody left to drive her, as her only child was already deceased, and most of her friends had already died or were barely alive as residents in nursing homes.

While they talked, the woman noticed that Hank was showing signs of discomfort, and convinced him to have a check-up at the free clinic himself. The doctor on duty there ran a series of tests and health screenings on Hank, and scheduled a biopsy for him as a result. Within a month, Hank was informed that he had cancer. He didn't think that life could have gotten any more difficult for him, but there he was, being handed a potential death sentence. Hank agreed to undergo an aggressive experimental treatment for it, and took the bus to the clinic every day after substitute teaching at nearby schools.

His treatments zapped the energy out of Hank, but he mustered up enough strength to start contacting each of his remaining friends via telephone, calling one per night, over the course of a week. The first call that he made was to Jenny.

"Hi Jenny, it's Hank," he said, upon hearing Jenny's voice on the other end of the line.

"Hank! Hey, your voice sounds different," Jenny said. "Is everything alright?"

"Well, not really," Hank began to explain," I was recently diagnosed with cancer."

"Oh, Hank. I'm so sorry," Jenny consoled. "But, you've got the strongest will out of everyone that I know, so I'm sure that you'll beat it, Hank."

"I sure hope so. They've got me on some experimental chemo."

"You'll be cancer-free in no time," Jenny suggested, even though she didn't know what form of cancer Hank had, or how aggressive it was.

"Jenny, I was hoping to get the gang together for a reunion at the frog pond over the next month or two. You're the first one I called, so let me know if there would be a week that works best for you."

"That sounds fun, Hank, but to be honest, I'll be tied up for the next six months, at least," Jenny said. "The wildlife sanctuary is undergoing some major changes, of which I am overseeing."

"What about coming up for just a weekend?" Hank hoped.

"I really wish I could, Hank, but Mickey Macaw has been sick, and I'd hate to leave him alone, even for just a weekend."

"Maybe your parents could bird-sit Mickey for a day or two?"

"I'm sorry Hank."

The next evening, Hank dialed Billy's number with hopes that he would be more available for a visit than Jenny was.

"Hank, my man! To what do I owe the honor?" Billy said, upon answering his phone.

"I wish I had better news, Billy. I was just diagnosed with cancer, and could really use a frog pond gang reunion," Hank responded, not wasting any time.

"Cancer? Look, that's a bummer, Hank, but there are so many ways to beat it today. Did they start you on chemotherapy?"

"Yes, and some other experimental drugs," Hank explained.

"Listen, there's a dude on the island who had cancer. He refused chemo, changed his diet to alkaline water and natural fruit and vegetable juicing, and he's still kicking today. Actually, add some music to that remedy because he attends almost all of our band's shows."

"Maybe you can tell me more about that in person. I'm hoping that the gang can unite at the frog pond, even for just one weekend, Billy. Would you be available to fly home over the next month or two?" Hank asked.

"Aww, man!" Billy started. "The band is completely booked every weekend for the next year."

"Not to minimize your contributions to the band, but maybe they could do the shows without a saxophone player for one weekend?

"I can't do that to the guys, Hank."

"But, they never had a sax player until you moved to the island, so it's not like they never did without one."

"Hank, that was a few decades ago. Most of our songs now revolve around the saxophone. As a matter of fact, I've even performed on days when I was really sick with a cold or the flu." Billy explained.

"I'd give anything to trade-in my sickness for a bout with a cold or the flu, instead," Hank uttered.

"You're the strongest person I know, Hank. You'll beat this, my friend."

"That's what Jenny said, too. Take care Billy, and good luck with the gigs," Hank stated, before hanging up the phone, disappointed.

Hank's treatments quite literally knocked him out for the few days that followed his conversation with Billy. Toward the end of that week, Hank felt well enough to make a phone call, and he dialed Grant's number.

"Hey Grant, it's Hank," he announced, when Grant answered the phone.

"Hank, how ya feeling, pal?" Grant asked, while he held the phone to his ear and watched the sunset from his lavish Martha's Vineyard home.

"Actually, I've got some-"

"Charlie told me that you were diagnosed with cancer," Grant interrupted. "It's going to take more than cancer to put a man like you down."

"I hadn't even spoken to Charlie yet. How did he know about my cancer?" Hank asked.

"I guess Benny told him about it." Grant answered.

"Benny? How the heck would Benny know anything about me at all these days?" Hank questioned, with a tinge of anger in his voice.

"My guess is that Jenny might have let him know, because she called me soon after I got off the phone with Charlie. She mentioned how you were hoping for a frog pond reunion, but everyone agreed that timing isn't really good for anyone right now, but hopefully next year."

"Everyone agreed? Who is everyone?" Hank asked, irritated.

"You know, the gang. Hank, I just bought the other two tour companies on Martha's Vineyard, so I need to be here to orchestrate and monitor the merge. Charlie's baby is keeping him busy, on top of him taking over the orchard now that his father-in-law has retired, and Billy-"

"I know about Billy," Hank quipped, "and Jenny, too."

"Hank, we'll definitely all get together when the timing works out best for everyone. Did I hear that you are riding the bus now?"

Hank remained quiet, as tears streamed from his eyes.

"Well, promise me that you'll kick this cancer's butt, brother."

"Yup", Hank said, knowing that his sorrow must have been evident while choking just to get out the one syllable before hanging up the phone.

His room was growing dark as the sun went down outside, and Hank made a mental note of how dark his life, also, was getting, when he previously believed that it couldn't get any darker. He felt too weak to stand up to turn on a light, so he pulled his legs up onto his air mattress and placed his head on his pillow. Hank tried to keep his mind as empty of any thoughts as possible, but he couldn't ignore the fact that his friends were calling each other and discussing how none of them had any interest in visiting Hank. Even worse, Hank couldn't believe that Grant and Charlie had already known, yet never even proactively called Hank upon hearing the news of his cancer. He kept waiting for a call from Charlie that never came, even months later.

For the next seven months, Hank went through the motions of life, choosing to teach classes at schools that were along the bus routes, and then afternoon treatments at the health clinic. The one bright spot in his life was a pretty woman that worked at the clinic who fell in love with Hank, and he with her. She'd give Hank rides home after his treatments so that he wouldn't need to take the bus in such a weak physical state. When Hank felt well enough to have company, she would stay with him for hours, and would sometimes spend the entire night, sleeping next to Hank on his air mattress. Aside from God, she was the best thing to have happened to Hank in a long time. She was also who Hank opened up to and spoke the most with, second only to God.

On the last day of that winter, Hank walked into the clinic after school and saw that his girlfriend's eyes looked puffy, as if she had been crying. She hardly made eye contact with Hank as she directed him to the doctor's personal office, instead of the usual lab where Hank would receive his treatments. By the time Hank left his office, he was in a state of shock. His girlfriend grabbed her keys to give Hank a ride home, but he explained to her that he needed the night to himself to process the news that he only had four to six months to live.

The next morning, he informed the school where he was scheduled to teach at that he wouldn't be in that day, and he headed straight for the frog pond, alone. It wasn't until he sat on top of the large stump near the frog pond, and overlooked the setting of his childhood, that reality hit him. Hank broke down and sobbed so hard that the colors and shapes of the trees and the frog pond blended together in a teardrop-induced kaleidoscope in his eyes. The shapes and colors danced in Hank's mind with an endless stream of memories that he and his friends made there.

Swirling around inside Hank's head were the sounds of each of his friend's voices, calling out each other's names when they would arrive at the frog pond. Hank could also hear the sweet tones of Billy's saxophone, birds chirping and singing, frogs croaking, Barnaby barking, airplane propellers overhead, and quarry blastings. He mentally replayed games of Hide-and-Seek, Rock Paper Scissors, and Cowboys-and-Indians. Hank was imagining the scents of blooming flowers, campfires, decaying leaves, baseball glove leather, bug spray, a freshly cut cedar tree branch, and the skunk cabbage that grew near the swampy area of the woods. He could taste the native blackberries that grew in the forest, the pie that Billy's mother made after a day of blueberry picking near Nine Men's Misery, peanut butter and jelly sandwiches, frozen treats from the ice cream truck on hot days, and various expired treats from the supermarket dumpster. He could feel the rough bark of the oak and maple trees, the smoothness of the beech trees, the slippery skin of the frogs and tadpoles, the wetness of the pond's water straining in-between fingers, and the cool softness of the field's grass under bare feet. Most of all, Hank could recall the feeling of love that he felt from his friends' hugs.

Hank remembered Barnaby chasing squirrels, and the time that one actually stopped and Barnaby ran right past it because he was running so fast and couldn't stop without sliding like he had stolen second base. When he finally did, he turned around and had a staring contest with the squirrel until they both just walked away.

He thought about Jenny reading books on the stump, which had to have been at least a hundred of them over the years at the frog pond. He laughed when he remembered the time that she tried to teach the others how to do a proper cartwheel.

Smiling when Terry came to mind, he could see him searching for bugs to add to his collection like it was just a day earlier, or the time that he showed the gang how to make firefly lanterns.

When thoughts of Billy were brought to Hank's mind, he saw him jumping his bike off ramps that he made out of plywood and milk crates, and the time that Billy tried to jump his bicycle over all of the metal Tonka trucks and Matchbox cars from the neighborhood, which resulted in five stitches under his chin. Hank also thought about the time that Billy wanted to prove to the others that there was a fox in the woods. He sat all day long, hanging onto a string that was tied to a stick about a hundred feet away, which was propping up a box with a ham sandwich under it for bait. Billy had demanded that nobody talked in the woods that day to give him a better chance at catching the fox, which never did show up for the sandwich. When the others started making jokes about Billy being a fox trapper, he said that the joke was on them, because he made them all Trappist Monks for the day as a result of them not being able to speak.

Hank's recollection of Charlie included him flying his remote controlled airplane over the field, doing loop-de-loops. He also remembered the time that Charlie taped sheets of Styrofoam to his arms and attempted to get himself airborne off the slope of the town's library lawn.

He remembered how Grant spent a week filming his own mini swamp creature film when he got a video camera for his birthday one year, and how everyone in the frog pond gang had an acting role in it. Hank vividly remembered how Grant would throw chunks of rock from the quarry into the pond during late summer when the water was covered green with algae. When the rock plunged into the pond, the algae would spread out in a large circle that exposed the water surface, and then slowly close the circular watery window, leaving no evidence that it ever even happened.

Hank cleared the kaleidoscope from his eyes and looked at the pond. Time had moved so fast, and there was no physical evidence left in the woods to suggest that his frog pond gang ever existed, except for a few carved trees near Nine Men's Misery, and the memories in his mind. While Hank sat there, he looked at the frog pond, and life, from a brand new angle, and a higher level of invigoration and appreciation. For the first time in his life, he had a general knowledge of the number of days he had left, which exponentially raised the value of each minute left for Hank to live. All of the memories that swam through his mind made it seem like his childhood was lived entirely within one long day, and what a glorious day it was, Hank thought, as he walked around the pond.

Hank then realized the gift from God that was in front of him. One more spring and summer, and then eternal life. He felt elation like he never felt before that morning. It was the first day of spring, and Hank was determined to make his last frog pond season the best season ever.

In his mind, he pictured Jenny's father counting One-Two-Three, and then Hank shouted as loud as he could, "WAKE UP FROGGIES!"

CHAPTER 9

The Best Season Ever

Hank continued to teach school for the remaining weeks of the school year, opting to take half-day assignments in the afternoon, as opposed to teaching full days. Every morning, he would prepare a travel mug of coffee and head out to the frog pond stump. Hank found that he had so many amazing memories of his life to reflect on that he could be entertained for hours while just sitting there, thinking and remembering. He inhaled the scents of the forest deeper than ever while he toggled back and forth between recalling memories, and thanking God for them in prayer. Hank also prayed for God's acceptance of him into Heaven. In between his thoughts, Hank would study the forest creatures around him more completely, contemplating the lives of grasshoppers, mosquitos, bees, ants, turtles, squirrels, birds, and of course, frogs. He wondered how many generations of them had come and gone without the frog pond gang ever even noticing while they lived among them.

After he taught school, his girlfriend, who also decided to work half-days to spend as much time with him as she could, would pick up Hank. They would spend a few hours each afternoon, walking throughout the woods, with Hank showing her every point of interest that most hikers would have simply walked past and missed. As they would walk, Hank felt lightness with each step, and a piece of mind like he had never experienced before. Even though his energy level was less than it was before his cancer diagnosis, he appreciated the fact that he didn't feel as tired as he did prior to telling the doctor that he would end his treatments and live out the rest of his days more naturally.

Once the school year ended, Hank spent two additional weeks of full days walking through the forest, sitting on the stump, and wrapping up all of his thoughts and memories with one last trip down each path. He understood the value of each and every footstep, and appreciated all of them, even as he stepped out of the frog pond woods for the very last time.

The announcement of Hank's death came as a mailed invitation to his funeral, shocking each of the friends who were still left of the frog pond gang that received one. The announcements arrived on the same day for all of the friends, prompting phone calls between each of them.

"I can't even believe that Hank is gone," Jenny said, crying into the phone to Grant. "I didn't expect him to die."

"None of us did," Grant responded. "I wonder why he didn't call us when he took a turn for the worst."

"Ugh. I just wish I found a way to get back home when he wanted to have a frog pond reunion."

"Well, it looks like we'll be seeing each other next week," Grant said, before dialing Billy's number.

"Dude, this is so surreal," Billy said, when he heard Grant's voice on the other end of the line. "I always thought that Hank would live forever, or at least outlive the rest of us."

"When will you be flying up for the funeral?" Grant asked.

"I'll probably arrive the day before. I already told the band that I'm going to miss all of our gigs next weekend."

"Charlie is calling on the other line. I'll see you next week, Billy," Grant said, before clicking over to Charlie's call. "Hey Charlie. I'm guessing that you received the notice about Hank's death, too."

"I feel so terrible," Charlie began, before bursting into tears. "I never even called him since learning that he had cancer. What an absolute jerk I am."

"Don't beat yourself up, Charlie. None of us expected Hank to die from it," Grant suggested.

"What do you make of the funeral invitation giving an R.S.V.P. phone number to the funeral home so we can donate to Hank's charity of choice, instead of sending flowers?" Charlie inquired.

"Yeah, I read that," Grant said. "I've never heard of the F.P.C. Foundation, but I'm guessing it's some sort of a cancer fund. I'm way overdue when it comes to giving to charity, so I'll call tomorrow with a large donation."

"Me, too," Charlie said. "I'll do the same. Well, I guess I'll be seeing you next week."

Jenny, Billy, Grant, and Charlie sat in the hotel restaurant and finished whatever they could choke down for breakfast. None of them had any appetite whatsoever, while they shared stories about Hank, and discussed the shame and regret that they felt for not being there for Hank while he was still alive.

Grant took care of the check, and Jenny called for a taxi van to pick them up and drive the four friends to the funeral home. Before they left the restaurant to wait outside for the taxi, Billy placed his hand over the middle of the table and suggested that they stack hands in a promise that they would all be there if anyone called for a reunion in the future, especially if they felt like they were dying. Everyone piled a hand upon Billy's and said "Amen", which surprised each of them as the word came out of their mouths.

Traffic was backed-up as the taxi neared the funeral home. Charlie could see a Ferris wheel towering over the church next door to it, and said, "It's ironic that Hank's funeral is the same day as the church carnival. He always loved them."

"Aww. We should all go over there after the service and ride the Ferris wheel in honor of Hank," Jenny suggested.

"I don't know," Grant said, as the taxi van pulled into the funeral home parking lot, "Hank was always afraid of heights. I see a carousel over there, too. Maybe we should ride that in memory of Hank, instead."

"Look! They have a game where you try to knock the bottles off the shelf with a baseball," Billy said. "I want to do that in honor of Hank."

Everyone's eyes began to well up as the taxi came to a stop.

"I so wish Hank was still here," Jenny said. "I miss him terribly, already."

The four friends were surprised to see that they were the only ones inside the funeral home, aside from the funeral director. They were directed to a viewing room off the far end of the hallway. Unlike their hikes through the woods, nobody was jockeying into position to be the leader into the room.

Grant was the first of them to walk over and kneel in front of the closed pewter-colored casket. Flowers that looked like clumps of snowflakes adorned the top of it, and its fragrance permeated the room, which added another layer of confirmation to their shocked and dulled senses that their friend's passing wasn't just a bad dream. Before he got up from kneeling to go sit on one of the seats, Grant read the card that was attached to the flowers. It said, "To Hank, our eternal friend. With love, from the Frog Pond Gang." Each of the friends took a turn to kneel in front of Hank's casket before taking a seat next to Grant.

"Who ordered the flowers?" Grant asked. "The funeral notice requested donations to a charity foundation in lieu of flowers."

"I couldn't resist," Jenny said. "I did make a donation, too, but Hank had bought me those same flowers when he visited me in Savannah. They are still growing in my courtyard."

Charlie took a glance around at all the empty chairs in the room and said, "I know that Hank wasn't doing so well over the past few years, having lost everything, and at least one friend that we know of during that time, but I figured there would be more people than this here. I mean, it's only us. Imagine if we didn't come in for the funeral?"

"What does losing all of his material things have to do with people not being here for his funeral?" Jenny asked.

"I think that's human nature," Charlie responded. "I mean, people begin to question those that lose everything, right?"

"I guess it's hard to hang out with others if you need to rely on public transportation to get around, unless you're living in a major city," Billy added. "It's just not the norm. Certainly, it would have been nearly impossible for him to have a girlfriend under those circumstances."

"Had he asked, I would have helped him, financially," Grant said.

"You know as well as the rest of us that Hank would never have asked for a handout, even if he were living under a bridge, cold and starving," Jenny responded.

The funeral director walked into the room, stood in front of the casket, and folded his hands.

Each of the friends sat at attention, expecting him to begin the funeral service.

"First, I'd like to take a moment to thank all of you for being here. Each and every one of us has a finite amount of time to walk upon the earth, and we recognize the sacrifice that you are making of your own personal time to be here. I must tell you that today's service will be a first for me. As you all know, Hank was very sick. He still is. I'm hoping that none of you will go into shock by what I'm about to tell you. Hank's life will be over within three months, but he didn't want to wait until he was dead to have his wake because he misses you all so much, and he wanted to say goodbye to you face to face. He realized that this approach would be the only way to make that happen. So, if you are ready, I'd like to bring Hank out here now."

Each of the friends looked at each other, wondering if they really heard what they thought they heard. The funeral director walked over to a side door, stuck his head inside, and then nodded. Charlie, Billy, Jenny, and Grant fixated their eyes on the doorway, and Hank appeared from around the corner. Jenny gasped when she saw how much weight he had lost.

"Please don't hate me for not being dead yet," Hank said, as he walked toward them.

"Oh, Hank!" Jenny said, while getting up and greeting him with a hug and a kiss. "We love you so much!"

The three others followed suit behind Jenny, and then Hank pulled up a chair and sat in front of them.

"Thanks so much for being here," Hank started. "I'm just going to talk for a minute or so, if you don't mind. This certainly isn't how I pictured the end of my life to go. I always envisioned an old man lying in that casket, many years from now. I pictured him to be a dignified man who was leaving behind an estate or two, some nice cars, a business, and maybe a yacht, which I would have left for all of you in my will. You'll find none of that to be the case. As you probably have heard, if I hadn't told you myself, I will be leaving this world with nothing but my soul, the same way each of us will. The difference with me is that I have nothing at all of value to leave behind. It is probably unfathomable to you that a man my age would have nothing to show for the years that he spent on earth. I know that I would feel that way, too, had it not happened to me.

All of my life, I had heard and read that one should give up their material things if a person is to truly follow God, and that it would be easier for a camel to pass through the eye of a needle than for a rich person to enter Heaven. I feel like I am perfectly positioned to meet God, even though I can't take credit for it. I was pretty much forced into this scenario, but now that I'm in it, I realize how much of a blessing my battle has been. If certain people hadn't betrayed me, I would have never been brought *this* close to God. I doubt that I would have given up all of my worldly possessions, and lived life in its most basic and primitive form by my own choosing. Through my struggles, I have met the most amazing people that I would otherwise never have interacted with. I would never have learned the lessons that I needed to learn had my life still been insulated from them because of me having all the material things I wanted or needed, or lacking any real personal battles. Actually, I thought that I had everything I needed, or even wanted. The truth is, all I ever needed was God, and the love of those around me. Nobody's love has meant more to me than the love I received from the frog pond gang, and I really want each of you to know how much I love you back. In addition to me wanting to spend one more day with you, I want you all to be at ease with my passing, and the way that I had to live my life over the past few years.

You all know how much I used to guard my reputation. I really did care what people thought about me, and considered that to be a gauge and reflection of how I was living my life. What I have learned over the past year, especially, is that I didn't need others' approvals of how I lived my life, but rather God's only. Maybe, sometimes, it's not that a person hit rock bottom, but rather humanity around him did. When I first started to ride the bus, I would hide my identity at all costs, with hopes that nobody in town knew how I was living. Once I realized what was important and real, I started feeling bad for all of those passing by in their cars that may not have been as in touch with the way God intended us to live. The freedom that I felt when I hit that realization was amazing. I took off the hood on my coat that I hid under and faced the street, and more importantly, prepared myself to face God.

Now, please know that I'm not being judgmental of any of you. I truly admire your talents, and the work that you've all done in your lives, so far. I can appreciate the rewards that you may be enjoying as a result of your hard work. I do hope that you sincerely enjoy the fruits of your labor, but if not, maybe consider peeling some away, layer by layer, until you reach the happiness layer, which is often derived from the spiritual layer. And if not, you may take comfort in the words Jesus said, which followed the camel and eye of a needle parable, which is "With man this is impossible, but with God all things are possible." I believe that, and I hope that all of you do, too.

Again, thank you so much for being here. I feel like a kid again. Today is one of the greatest gifts of my life because I get to share it with you. For me, this is a very special last day with the frog pond gang that I didn't think I'd live to see."

"Hank, I think that I can speak for the entire gang when I say thank you for doing this today," Billy said.

"Yes, thank you, Hank. And I'm sorry for not reaching out to you like I should have over the past year," Charlie added.

"I honestly get it. I hope that you brought photos of the new baby, Charlie," Hank responded.

"I sure did!" Charlie affirmed.

"You really are amazing, Hank," Jenny said. "I hope that you realize how much we all love you."

"You're giving us a special gift today, Hank," Grant confirmed. "How would you like to spend it together?"

"Thanks to all of you, we get to have a carnival today," Hank answered.

"You'd like to spend it at the church carnival? That sounds like fun!" Jenny said.

"The church gave us the land for the day, but the carnival is ours," Hank stated.

"I'm not following," Charlie said.

"You each donated to the F.P.C. Foundation, which stands for the Frog Pond Carnival Foundation. We always talked about having our own carnival, and giving back through it, and today we are making it a reality."

"That's so cool," Billy responded.

"How is it that it gives back?" Grant asked.

"You'll see when we get out there." Hank answered.

"What happens after today, Hank?" Jenny asked, with concern in her voice.

"Well, tomorrow will be more like a real wake here at the funeral home. That's where you'll get to say goodbye, like all of us wanted to do at Terry's funeral. From there, I will leave to live my final weeks in a small cottage that my girlfriend and I rented in a secret location."

"You've got a new girl, Hank?" Grant asked.

"I do. She works at the health clinic. We had talked about someday escaping to a small cottage somewhere, once I won my battle against cancer. Since the disease sucker-punched me, we decided to do the cottage thing anyway, and try to pack a year's worth of love and life into each and every day there. The doctor was very understanding, and he gave her a leave of absence until my passing."

"Boy, you sure know how to do death, Hank," Charlie said.

"We'll all do it eventually," Hank replied. "Come on, let's go live while we're all still here."

Hank led the gang across the parking lot to the large field behind the church where all of the rides, games, and carnival food stands were set up. Bells were ringing, lights were blinking, kids were laughing, and the frog pond gang's faces were lit up with huge smiles.

"This is spectacular, Hank!" Jenny said.

"Who are these people?" Charlie asked. "There must be a few hundred kids and their parents here."

"A lot of them are students from the inner-city schools that I teach at. Most of these kids have never experienced a carnival because of the typical costs. Today, they can ride all the rides, play all of the games, win prizes, and eat whatever they want to, all day long for free, because of each of you."

A public bus pulled into the parking lot, dropping off more families to enjoy the carnival. A frail woman wearing very old clothes got off the bus with two children and headed straight for Hank.

"Thank you so much for doing this for us, Hank," the woman said. "My grandchildren have never been this excited."

"You're welcome, Millie," Hank replied. "We owe all the thanks to my four best friends that are with us today, and to God for allowing it to come together so perfectly."

"Well, we're sure going to miss you when you're gone, Hank. The bus won't be the same without you on it," the woman said, before heading to the carousel, being led by the two thrilled children who were pulling her by her hands.

"More students?" Grant asked, catching up to them and distributing five doughboys.

No, Millie rides the bus, and most people that do just don't have the means to take their families to carnivals, so lots of these folks today are people who I've met on the bus, too."

"If you don't mind me asking, how did you break the news to all of your students and fellow bus riders?" Jenny asked.

"I didn't," Hank said. "Everyone just thinks that I am moving away, which is actually the truth, and that this is a going away carnival."

The frog pond gang spent the next several hours riding, playing, laughing, and at times, crying, especially when they stopped at the dunk tank, which evoked some of their earliest memories. It broke their hearts to watch Hank get winded from throwing the baseball at the target during his three chances.

Hank rode with the others on the Ferris wheel, explaining to them that there was nothing left for him to fear, as he looked around in every direction with a big smile on his face whenever he approached the wheel's highest point, and giggled from the sensation in his tummy as the wheel took him back down. Hank's four best friends had an even deeper appreciation for their most loyal childhood friend, as they witnessed no less than a hundred kids go up to Hank to give hugs, high-fives, or to proudly show him a prize that they won by playing one of the carnival games. At the end of the day, Hank's four closest friends felt like the biggest winners overall, with having spent one of the most special of days with the most special person they knew, their friend Hank.

Eventually, Hank needed to announce that he had one of his best days ever, and the very best life, with the best friends that any human could have imagined, but that he felt like he needed to sleep, and explained that he would be picked up by his girlfriend soon. He informed them that the wake would begin at ten o'clock in the morning, with the heads-up that it would have an entirely different mood than their carnival day. He told each of them that he loved them so very much, while he hugged them, one by one, for a good long time.

Hank was pleased that the sun was shining down on his last day in town. His girlfriend's car was already packed, and as she drove Hank to the funeral home, they reviewed everything that they were taking with them to their secret cottage, making sure that they didn't forget anything. The carnival crew was disassembling the rides and games in the field next door to the funeral home when Hank's girlfriend pulled up in front of the door. He thanked her for the ride, and for understanding why he wanted to have the private wake with just his frog pond gang in attendance. Hank kissed her cheek and then got ready to open his door when he noticed a white, air-dancing tube-man, bending down toward the car and snapping back with its arms flailing.

"Did you just nod to that thing?" Hank's girlfriend asked.

Hank turned his head back toward her with the biggest smile that she ever saw on his face, and said, "I sure did!"

Jenny, Charlie, Billy and Grant arrived together, just before ten o'clock, a half hour after Hank had arrived. They were greeted at the door by the funeral director, who brought them into one of the front rooms, first, to explain how Hank wanted his wake to be conducted. He told them that each of them would have a private moment at the casket, at which time they could say goodbye to Hank. The director informed them that Hank would be laying in the casket with his eyes closed, and that he'd be able to listen to them, but wouldn't be responding. It was Hank's wish that it would be as authentic a wake as possible.

When one of the friends expressed disappointment that Hank wasn't ever going to speak to them again, the funeral director reminded them of the gift that Hank gave to all of them the day before. He said that if Hank had already passed away before he was able to orchestrate the reunion of the gang, not only would he be non-speaking, he wouldn't be hearing, either. He added that Hank's approach allowed them some real closure, as compared to their friend Terry's funeral a few years earlier. He also went on to say that Hank did leave lengthy letters for each of the frog pond friends, which they would be receiving at the conclusion of the wake. The friends were relieved to hear that, and also that they would be able to hold Hank's hands during their goodbyes to him.

The funeral director left the friends alone in the room together so they could have a moment to gather their thoughts before kneeling in front of their friend to say goodbye for the final time.

"I'm just not ready for this," Billy said.

"Will there ever be a time when any of us will actually be ready?" Grant asked. "I'll admit that I have butterflies in my stomach."

"I think that we all agree that Hank was pretty much THE best friend to each one of us," Jenny suggested. "We really owe it to him for us to be brave, and share with him our thoughts so that he feels nothing but love when he leaves here."

"I agree, Jenny," Charlie responded. "What do you say we do 'Rock Paper Scissors' for old-time's sake to see which order we go in to give our final respects and goodbyes to Hank?"

Billy was the first of the friends to walk into the funeral home's viewing room. He could feel his heart beating out of his chest as he slowly walked past collages of photos of Hank and the gang that rested on several easels. Reliving moments that he had long forgotten about. Billy began to feel the reality with each tear that clung to his cheeks while he tried to cling onto what was left of Hank's physical existence on earth.

Billy looked over toward the casket and could see the back of Hank's head while he inched his way toward him, hoping that Hank couldn't hear any evidence of his sobbing. Billy stopped for an uncomfortable amount of time, until he felt strong enough to say words to Hank without breaking down. Trying to focus on something else in effort to keep his composure, Billy took a mental note of how comfortable the carpet felt under his dress shoes. Having been living a life on an island, Billy had little use for fancy shoes, unless he was performing at a wedding. But, through the soles of them, the carpet felt to Billy as if he were walking on a cloud as he walked around to the front of the casket, and kneeled down.

Hank was dressed in a perfectly fitted suit, which was given to him by the tailor who owned a clothing shop near one of Hank's bus stops. While waiting for his bus, Hank would gaze at that particular suit in the window. He really liked it, knowing he would need an outfit to wear for his wake, but also knowing that it was way outside of his budget. When his girlfriend secretly visited the clothing store one afternoon to put some money down on it with hopes of surprising Hank by giving it to him as a gift, the owner learned about Hank's fate and donated it to him then and there.

"Hank, it's me, Billy. Man, I just want to thank you for being the absolute best friend I could have ever imagined. You were always the first to believe in me, and the last one to judge. That having been said, you did always have words of wisdom to share, whatever the situation was." Billy began.

He paused for a few seconds to see if Hank would have any response or reaction. He did not, but rather remained stoic inside his casket with his hands folded over his chest, and his eyes remaining closed. During that pause, Billy noticed that there was music playing through the funeral home's speaker system, and it happened to be very familiar music to him, indeed.

"Wait," Billy continued. "Is that my newest recording playing right now? You really are something, Hank, having supported my music throughout all of these years. Next to my mother, nobody cheered me on as much as you did. From this moment forward, I am going to dedicate a song to my friend Hank during every single gig I play, until I'm in one of these caskets myself. In addition to that, I should tell you that the hotel where you always stayed at while visiting me on the island has named their most popular drink after you. It's called 'Hank's Fastball', and they serve it in a coconut."

Billy noticed Hank smile, which made him smile, too, just as another teardrop fell.

"Well, the others want to say goodbye, also. I love you Hank," Billy said, just before touching Hank's hands. Hank grabbed Billy's hand with both of his, held it for several seconds, and then let go. Billy walked away from the casket in tears, and sat on one of the chairs in the room.

Grant was the next of the friends to enter the room. He took time to look at all of the displayed photos before kneeling in front of Hank's casket. Glancing over at Billy, whose face was red and swollen from crying, Grant thought to himself that he wanted to keep himself together better than that. Facing Hank, he cleared his throat and began to talk.

"You look sharp, Hank," Grant said, and then waited for a reaction, but received not one flinch from Hank. "I was looking at the picture over there of us at the beach when we were kids. I'll never forget the day that you hid me on the floor in the back seat of your mother's car under a blanket. You knew that she'd say there was no room in the car to take a friend with your family to the beach, and only announced that I was in the car once it was too far for her to have turned around to drop me back off. You cared so much for all of us friends, and that was just one example out of hundreds, knowing that I'd otherwise have to spend that summer day at home, alone. I'll tell you, if I could make a U-turn and relive our lives, I wouldn't change a thing, especially my friendship with you, Hank."

Grant paused and looked back over at Billy, wondering if he could hear him speak or not. He considered the saxophone music playing in the room, and figured that Billy would only be able to hear mumbling from where he sat, if he could hear anything at all.

"Hank, I've got to say that you helped me out more than you know when I was going through my breakdown. Your perspective on things helped me to realize what was important, and what wasn't. You may be leaving the world with less than any of us, but I see you as the wealthiest among the gang. Respect is not something that anyone can buy with money. I could always see how much respect you were earning over the decades, but yesterday blew me away when I saw how all of those people at the carnival were looking up to you. It was proof of sincere love, which is something that the largest of bank accounts couldn't purchase. What a large bank account *can* invest in, though, is the F.P.C. Foundation. I made a decision last night to make the carnival a weeklong annual event to benefit the poorest and most needy people, just like you organized yesterday. It will be called Hank's Frog

Pond Carnival, and the trust fund that I am setting up for it will ensure that the carnival will run for decades longer than any of the frog pond gang will live. Well, it sure is hard to say goodbye, Hank, but I will never ever forget you, or anything that you've ever done for me. Say hi to Terry for me."

Hank lifted a hand off his chest for a handshake. Grant shook it with both of his hands, and with watery eyes, headed away from the casket to take a seat next to Billy.

Charlie stepped into the room and walked straight over to Hank's casket, falling to his knees and folding his hands. He bowed his head down with his eyes closed for a moment, and then raised his head and looked at Hank's face. "I've got to thank you, Hank," Charlie started. "When you came out for the wedding, I told you that I didn't believe in God and you basically pleaded with me to give God another chance. Well, when my daughter was being born seven months later, there were complications with the birth and the doctor was fairly certain that we were going to lose her. Your words kept echoing in my head, and I headed directly to the chapel that was in the hospital. While I was in there, I asked that if there was a God, that he would hear my requests to save my daughter. During my prayers, I apologized for having fallen away from Him, and promised that I would get closer to Him. I even suggested that if I hadn't had enough faith over the years to ask for such a miracle, that I was sure that my friend Hank would let me borrow some from his spiritual bank, and that I'd pay him back. Well, the miracle happened, and she is perfectly healthy today. As for me, I've become involved in the local church, and have a hunger to walk with God like I never thought would be possible for me."

Hank flashed a visible smile.

Charlie looked back over at Grant and Billy for a second before he continued to speak. "I'm going to share some news with you, Hank, that the others aren't aware of yet. My wife and I are expecting our second child. She went for an ultrasound yesterday, and called me at the hotel last night to inform me that we will be having a boy. We both decided that his name will be Henry, in honor of you."

Hank raised his hands and Charlie held onto them for several seconds before heading toward his seat. After taking a few steps, he stopped, turned around, and headed back toward the casket.

"I just want to let you know, if you ever see me flying my airplane straight up toward Heaven, I'm not trying to stall it, but rather just trying to get a little closer to you. I love you, Hank."

Jenny was already crying when she walked into the room. She spent several minutes looking at the collages of pictures. Charlie walked over to look at them with her, rubbing her back for support. When they got to the last easel of photos, Charlie kissed Jenny on her head and took a seat so she could have her moment with Hank.

She kneeled down and took hold of Hank's hands right away. At first, she only cried. Eventually, she regained enough of her composure to begin speaking to Hank.

"Oh Hank. Saying goodbye to you is the hardest thing I've ever had to do. Whether it would have come years ago like Terry, or decades from now like that elderly couple we met in Savannah, this is a day that I have dreaded since the first year that we were friends. There was just something about you that made life on earth better, and I was blessed with every day that God kept you here. Now that He is taking you back, I want to confess that the reason why I never got married was because I could never find a man that came close to measuring up to you. You were my benchmark for the perfect man."

Jenny peered over at Grant, Billy and Charlie, during a quick pause before continuing.

"I've always loved you, Hank, and I think I *fell* in love with you at that fountain in Savannah, when I witnessed an example of true love between life-long friends as I watched the elder couple. As a matter of fact, my bird Mickey Macaw now says, "I love Hank," over and over. I'm sure that he'll be saying that for the rest of his life, as will I."

Hank felt around Jenny's hands until he located her ring finger, and pretended to slip a ring onto it.

"I do," Jenny said, before leaning over to give Hank a kiss before joining the others on the seats.

Knowing that all four friends had said their goodbyes, Hank folded his hands and recited The Lord's Prayer in his mind.

"Our Father which art in heaven, hallowed be thy name. Thy kingdom come. Thy will be done, on earth as it is in heaven. Give us this day our daily bread. And forgive us our trespasses, as we forgive those that trespass against us. And lead us not into temptation, but deliver us from evil."

When he finished, he heard creaking from the pedestal where everyone kneeled in front of his casket. Hank thought that the funeral director was going to pay his respects before closing out the service, but the voice Hank heard didn't come from the director.

"I'm so sorry, Hank," Benny said, while kneeling in front of Hank's casket.

Hank sat up and hugged his friend Benny. The rest of the frog pond gang got out of their seats and joined in on a group hug. There was a mixture of crying and laughing, sadness and happiness. Eventually, Benny felt Hank's body give in to his weakness, and he gently rested his friend back down onto the pillow.

While the frog pond gang stood over him, Hank stuck a hand outside of the casket, and said, "Let's stack hands, that when it's your time to come, you'll follow me along the path to Heaven for the best season ever."

Jenny placed a hand on top of Hank's.
Grant placed a hand on top of Jenny's.
Billy placed a hand on top of Grant's.
Benny placed a hand on top of Billy's.
Charlie placed a hand on top of Benny's.
"AMEN!"

For God so loved the world that he gave
his one and only Son, that whoever believes in
him shall not perish but have eternal life.

John 3:16

Please read THE BIBLE next

Additional suggested books,
written by Joe Silva:

'ST. PURGATORY'

'A JOURNEY THROUGH A DREAM'

www.TheJoeSilvaWebsite.com

Frogs, Friends, & Funerals

Frogs, Friends, & Funerals

Made in the USA
Middletown, DE
01 October 2020